NEURODIVERGENT TEENS

12 Success Stories of Teens with ADHD and Autism Who Learned to Thrive—With Proven Strategies, Weekly Action Plans, and Reflection Exercises for Every Challenge

By Richard Bass

COPYRIGHT

Neurodivergent Teens: 12 Success Stories of Teens with ADHD and Autism Who Learned to Thrive—With Proven Strategies, Weekly Action Plans, and Reflection Exercises for Every Challenge

While the author holds bachelor's and master's degrees in education along with certifications in Special Education (K–12) and Educational Administration, this book does not constitute professional medical or therapeutic advice. The strategies and information presented are based on research, educational best practices, and the collective experiences of the neurodivergent community, but they are not a substitute for individualized professional guidance.

Medical and Mental Health Disclaimer:

This book discusses neurodevelopmental conditions including ADHD, autism, dyslexia, and related challenges. The stories presented are fictionalized composites for educational purposes and are not based on specific real individuals. Any resemblance to actual persons, living or deceased, is purely coincidental.

No diagnosis can or should be made based on the content of this book. If you believe you or your child may be neurodivergent, please consult with qualified healthcare professionals including licensed psychologists, psychiatrists, developmental pediatricians, or other medical specialists who can conduct comprehensive evaluations.

Never start, stop, or modify any medication or treatment plan without consulting your healthcare provider. Any discussion of medication, therapy, or interventions in this book is for informational purposes only.

If you or someone you know is experiencing a mental health crisis, suicidal thoughts, or severe distress, please seek immediate help:

- National Suicide Prevention Lifeline: 988
- Crisis Text Line: Text HOME to 741741
- Emergency Services: 911

Educational Rights Disclaimer:

While this book discusses educational accommodations, IEPs, 504 plans, and disability rights, it does not constitute legal advice. Educational law varies by location, and specific situations require consultation with special education advocates, attorneys, or professionals familiar with disability law in your jurisdiction.

Liability Waiver:

By reading this document, the reader agrees that under no circumstances is the author or publisher responsible for any losses, direct or indirect, that are incurred as a result of the use of information contained within this document, including, but not limited to, errors, omissions, or inaccuracies. The reader assumes full responsibility for how they choose to use the information presented.

The content within this book has been derived from various sources including educational research, clinical studies, and lived experiences within the neurodivergent community. Readers should consult licensed professionals before implementing any techniques, strategies, or recommendations outlined in this book, particularly those involving children, mental health, education, or medical decisions.

Acknowledgment of Diversity:

The neurodivergent community is diverse, and experiences vary widely among individuals. This book attempts to represent common patterns and challenges but cannot encompass every unique experience. If your experience differs from what is described, that does not invalidate your reality or the legitimacy of your needs.

A NOTE TO READERS

Who This Book Is For

This book is written primarily for **neurodivergent teens** (ages 13-18) who are navigating life with ADHD, autism, dyslexia, or other neurodevelopmental differences. If you've ever felt:

- Different from your peers in ways you can't quite explain
- Exhausted from trying to appear "normal"
- Confused about why things that seem easy for others are hard for you
- Alone in your struggles with focus, social situations, sensory input, or emotional regulation
- Misunderstood by parents, teachers, or friends
- Curious about what diagnosis means or whether you might be neurodivergent

This book is for you.

However, this book is also valuable for:

- **Parents** who want to better understand their neurodivergent teen's lived experience

- **Educators** who work with neurodivergent students and want insight into their internal world
- **Siblings** and **friends** of neurodivergent teens who want to be more supportive
- **Newly diagnosed adults** who wish they'd had this resource as teens
- **Therapists and counselors** who work with neurodivergent adolescents

How to Use This Book

This is not a book you have to read cover-to-cover in order (though you can if you want to). Each of the twelve stories stands alone, so feel free to:

- **Jump to the story that resonates most** with your current challenge
- **Read one story at a time** and work through the reflection questions and action steps before moving on
- **Share specific stories** with parents, friends, or teachers who need to understand your experience
- **Revisit stories** as you face new challenges or reach new stages in your neurodivergent journey
- **Use the action steps** as practical tools whenever you need them

Content Notes

This book discusses:

- Mental health challenges including anxiety, depression, and burnout
- Masking and its emotional toll
- Social rejection and bullying (not graphically described)
- Family conflict and misunderstanding
- Academic struggles and feelings of inadequacy
- Meltdowns, shutdowns, and sensory overwhelm

- Diagnosis experiences (including both positive and
  difficult aspects)

If any of these topics are particularly difficult for you right now, it's okay to skip those sections or read them when you feel ready. Your mental health comes first.

A Promise

This book will not:

- Tell you how to "overcome" or "fix" your neurodivergence
- Suggest that you need to become more neurotypical to be successful
- Shame you for needing accommodations or struggling with things others find easy
- Present neurodivergence as purely tragic or purely a "superpower"

This book will:

- Validate your real experiences and challenges
- Provide practical strategies that actually work for neurodivergent brains
- Help you understand why certain things are hard (and that it's not your fault)
- Show you that you're not alone—millions of teens share your struggles
- Empower you to advocate for yourself and build a life that works with your brain, not against it

You deserve to understand yourself. You deserve to be understood. You deserve support, accommodations, and acceptance.

Let's begin.

DEDICATION

To every neurodivergent teen who has been told they're "too much" or "not enough"—
You are exactly right.
To the teens who mask until they can't anymore, who stim in bathroom stalls, who spend hours researching their neurodivergence online, who advocate for themselves when adults dismiss their needs, who support each other in spaces not built for them, who are building a better, more accepting world—
This book is for you.
You are not broken. You are not alone. You are not failing at being human. Your brain works differently. And that's not just okay—it's valuable.
Keep going. Your tribe is waiting.

TABLE OF CONTENTS

INTRODUCTION

Hey.

If you picked up this book, there's a good chance you've been told your brain works differently. Maybe you have ADHD, autism, dyslexia, dyspraxia, or another form of neurodivergence. Maybe you've known this about yourself for years, or maybe you just found out recently. Either way, you're probably tired of books that treat neurodivergence like a problem to be fixed or a deficit to overcome.

This isn't that kind of book.

What This Book Is

This is a collection of stories about teenagers whose brains work differently—and who are figuring out how to thrive, not despite their neurodivergence, but often because of the unique perspectives and strengths it gives them.

These characters aren't inspirational superheroes who overcome their disabilities through sheer willpower. They're real kids dealing with real challenges: sensory overload at school, executive function struggles, social confusion, rejection sensitive dysphoria, and the exhaustion of masking who they really are.

But they're also discovering their strengths: deep focus on special interests, pattern recognition, creative problem-solving, intense loyalty, and authentic ways of being in the world that neurotypical people sometimes miss.

Most importantly, they're learning that accommodations aren't cheating, stimming isn't shameful, and needing support doesn't make you weak.

What This Book Isn't

This book isn't:

- A medical guide or diagnostic tool
- A cure or treatment plan
- Written by someone who thinks you need to be "fixed"
- Full of inspiration porn about "overcoming" disability
- A one-size-fits-all instruction manual

Every neurodivergent person is different. Your ADHD doesn't look like your friend's ADHD. Your autism doesn't look like the autism you see in movies. Your sensory needs are unique to you.

So while these stories might feel familiar in some ways, they're not meant to represent every possible neurodivergent experience. They're windows into fifteen different lives, each showing one way of being neurodivergent in today's world.

How This Book Works

Each chapter contains:

A Story - About a neurodivergent teenager navigating a specific challenge or discovery. The characters are diverse in their neurodivergence, backgrounds, interests, and experiences.

Reflect - Questions to help you think about how the story connects to your own life. There are no right or wrong answers—just honest reflection.

Act - A practical challenge or activity that takes the story's theme and helps you apply it to your own situation. These aren't homework assignments. They're invitations to experiment with new ways of understanding yourself and navigating the world.

How to Use This Book

There's no required reading order. You can:

- Read straight through from beginning to end
- Jump to stories that address challenges you're currently facing
- Read one story, try the activity, and come back when you're ready for more
- Share specific stories with parents, teachers, or friends who might benefit from understanding your experience
- Revisit stories that hit differently as you grow and change

The only wrong way to use this book is to read it expecting easy answers or quick fixes. Neurodivergence isn't something you solve—it's something you understand, accommodate, and increasingly, celebrate.

A Note About Language

You'll notice this book uses identity-first language ("autistic person") rather than person-first language ("person with autism"). This reflects the preference of many neurodivergent people who see their neurodivergence as an integral part of who they are, not something separate that they "have."

That said, language preferences are personal. If you prefer different terminology for yourself, that's completely valid. Use whatever language feels right for you.

The Neurodivergent Experience in 2025

Being a neurodivergent teenager in 2025 is complicated. On one hand, there's more awareness and acceptance than ever before. The neurodiversity movement has created communities where differences are celebrated rather than pathologized. Online spaces allow you to connect with other neurodivergent people who just get it without explanation.

On the other hand, schools are still designed for neurotypical brains. Social expectations often don't account for different communication styles. The pressure to mask—to hide your neurodivergent traits to fit in—is real and exhausting.

These stories acknowledge both realities: the progress that's been made and the challenges that remain. They show characters navigating systems that weren't built for them, while also finding spaces where they can be authentically themselves.

What Makes You Neurodivergent Makes You, You

Here's something important that runs through all these stories: your neurodivergence isn't a bug in your system that needs to be patched. It's a different operating system entirely—one with its own logic, strengths, and ways of processing the world.

Yes, that different operating system can create challenges in a world designed for a different OS. And yes, you'll need to develop strategies, accommodations, and support systems to navigate those challenges.

But you'll also discover that your neurodivergent brain gives you perspectives and abilities that neurotypical people might miss:

- Seeing patterns others overlook
- Bringing intense focus to things that fascinate you
- Thinking outside boxes that others don't even see as boxes
- Experiencing emotions and sensory input with remarkable depth
- Creating innovative solutions precisely because you approach problems differently

The goal isn't to become less neurodivergent. The goal is to understand your brain well enough to advocate for what you need, build on your strengths, and find environments and people who appreciate you for who you actually are.

You're Not Alone

One of the hardest parts of being neurodivergent is feeling like you're the only one who struggles with things that seem easy for everyone else. Like you're the only one who finds crowded hallways overwhelming, or conversations exhausting, or time management impossible, or emotional regulation mysterious.

But you're not alone. Millions of teenagers have brains that work like yours. Many of them feel just as isolated, confused, or frustrated as you might feel sometimes.

These stories are meant to remind you that:

- Your challenges are real and legitimate
- Your experiences are valid
- Your needs deserve to be met
- Your differences are not deficits
- Your neurodivergent community is out there, waiting to welcome you

A Word of Encouragement

Being a teenager is hard. Being a neurodivergent teenager in a neurotypical world is even harder. You're dealing with all the regular challenges of adolescence—identity questions, social dynamics, academic pressure, family relationships—while also navigating sensory sensitivities, executive function struggles, social communication differences, and the exhaustion of constantly translating between your world and the neurotypical world.

That's a lot to carry.

But you're carrying it. You're here. You're reading this book because some part of you wants to understand yourself better, connect with others who share your experience, or find new strategies for thriving in a world that doesn't always accommodate your needs.

That desire to understand and grow—that's strength, not weakness.

The characters in these stories aren't perfect. They make mistakes, struggle with self-acceptance, and sometimes wish their brains worked differently. But they also learn to appreciate their unique ways of experiencing the world. They find their people. They develop strategies that work for them. They advocate for themselves, even when it's scary.

You can do those things too.

Your Story Continues

These fifteen stories are just snapshots—moments in the lives of neurodivergent teenagers figuring things out. Your story is ongoing, with many chapters yet to be written.

Some of those chapters will be hard. You'll face teachers who don't understand, peers who don't accept, and systems that weren't designed for you. You'll have days when you wish your brain came with a manual or worked like everyone else's.

But you'll also have moments of profound connection with people who truly get you. You'll discover strengths you didn't know you had. You'll find communities where your differences are celebrated. You'll learn that the things that make life harder in some ways also make it richer in others.

Your neurodivergence is part of your story, but it's not the whole story. You're also a person with interests, dreams, relationships, struggles, and strengths that have nothing to do with how your brain is wired.

These stories honor both truths: your neurodivergence shapes your experience of the world, and you're so much more than your neurodivergence.

Let's Begin

The teenagers you're about to meet are fictional, but the experiences they're navigating are real. The challenges they face are ones that neurodivergent teens encounter every day. The discoveries they make are ones that might resonate with your own journey.

1

———

THE MASK COMES OFF

Emma adjusted her expression in the bathroom mirror before heading to lunch. Smile—not too big, that looked fake. Not too small, that looked unfriendly. Somewhere in between. Natural, but not too natural because her actual natural expression apparently made her look "mad" or "bored."

She'd been practicing faces since she was twelve, when her mom gently suggested that she might want to "work on her social skills." What that really meant was: learn to pretend you're someone else so people will like you better.

At sixteen, Emma had become an expert at masking. She knew exactly how long to maintain eye contact (too little seemed rude, too much seemed intense). She knew which laugh to use for which social situation. She knew how to force herself to eat lunch in the crowded cafeteria even when the noise made her want to scream. She knew how to nod along when her friends discussed things she didn't care about, pretending to be interested in whatever drama was unfolding this week.

She was so good at masking that most people had no idea she was autistic. Teachers praised her for being "high-functioning" (a term she'd learned to hate). Friends told her she "didn't seem autistic" (which was not the compliment they thought it was). Even her parents sometimes forgot, suggesting she should "just try harder" when she struggled with things that came naturally to neurotypical people.

The mask worked. It protected her from bullying, from exclusion, from being seen as "weird" or "difficult." But it was also exhausting her in ways she was only beginning to understand.

Emma took a deep breath, fixed her smile one more time, and headed to lunch.

THE CAFETERIA WAS its usual sensory nightmare—hundreds of conversations layered on top of each other, fluorescent lights flickering overhead, the smell of grease and sanitizer mixing together. Emma's shoulders tensed automatically, but she forced them down. Relaxed. Casual. Normal.

"Emma! Over here!" Sarah waved from their usual table.

Emma navigated through the crowd, careful not to bump into anyone, hyperaware of the social choreography required to move through a packed space. She slid into her seat next to Maya and across from Sarah and Jenna.

"So, did you hear about what happened between Marcus and Destiny?" Sarah launched immediately into a story Emma had already heard three times that morning.

Emma nodded, made the appropriate facial expressions, inserted the occasional "oh my god" or "no way" at the right moments. Inside, she was counting down the minutes until lunch ended and she could go to the library, where it was quiet and she could just be herself for twenty minutes.

"Emma, are you even listening?" Jenna asked.

Emma snapped back to attention. She'd zoned out again, staring at the pattern of the table while Sarah talked. "Sorry, yeah, I'm listening."

"You've been so spacey lately," Sarah said, sounding annoyed. "Is everything okay?"

"I'm fine," Emma said automatically. "Just tired."

It wasn't a lie. She was tired—exhausted, actually. But it wasn't the kind of tired that sleep could fix. It was the bone-deep exhaustion of spending every waking hour performing a version of herself that other people found acceptable.

THAT EVENING, Emma logged into her favorite online game, a fantasy MMORPG where she'd been playing for two years. Gaming was her sanctuary. Behind her avatar, she could focus on quests and strategy without worrying about facial expressions or appropriate small talk.

She joined her guild's voice chat for a raid. Usually, she kept her mic muted, communicating only through text. But tonight, the raid leader was coordinating complex battle strategies, and text wasn't fast enough.

"Emma, can you get on voice?" her guild leader, Luna, asked. "We need quick callouts for this boss fight."

Emma hesitated, then unmuted. "Okay, I'm here."

They launched into the raid. Emma focused entirely on the mechanics—dodge this attack, interrupt that spell, position here. When she was absorbed in the game, she forgot to monitor herself. Her communication was direct, efficient, literal. No social niceties, just pure information exchange.

"Boss turning east, ranged move left," Emma called out.

"Interrupt ready in five, four, three, two, one, interrupting now."

"That mechanic makes no sense, the hitbox is completely incon-sistent with the visual indicator."

The raid went smoothly. Afterward, Luna messaged her privately.

Luna: Hey, that was great! You're really good at callouts. Why don't you talk more often?

Emma: I don't know. I guess I'm usually too anxious.

Luna: Anxious about what?

Emma paused. Behind the safety of text, she found herself being honest in a way she never was at school.

Emma: About saying the wrong thing or sounding weird. I'm autistic and I never know if I'm communicating the way people expect.

She held her breath, waiting for Luna's response. This was exactly why she didn't tell people.

Luna: Oh cool, me too! I'm autistic as well. That explains why your communication style felt so refreshing—very direct and clear. No unnecessary filler.

Emma stared at her screen. Someone thought her communication style was *refreshing*?

Luna: Is this the first time you've told someone in the guild?

Emma: Is it that obvious that I don't usually tell people?

Luna: Let me guess—you mask a lot in real life?

Emma: How did you know?

Luna: Because I do too. Different brains, different strengths.

Emma sat back in her chair, processing this. Here was someone who not only knew she was autistic but saw it as a neutral fact—maybe even a positive one—rather than something to overcome or hide.

Emma: Can I ask you something? Do you mask? Like, act neurotypical to fit in?

Luna: Oh absolutely. Especially at work and with my family. It's exhausting though. That's part of why I love gaming—I can unmask here.

Emma: Same. I mask all day at school. By the time I get home, I'm completely drained.

Luna: Have you heard of autistic burnout?

Emma hadn't, so Luna sent her several links to articles and blog posts written by autistic adults about the cumulative exhaustion of constant masking. Reading them felt like someone had finally put words to what Emma had been experiencing for years.

OVER THE NEXT FEW WEEKS, Emma found herself spending more time talking with Luna, not just about game strategy but about their experiences being neurodivergent. Luna introduced her to other neurodivergent members of their guild, and Emma discovered a community of people who understood her without explanation.

For the first time in years, Emma had a space where she could truly relax. Where she didn't have to monitor her tone or facial expressions. Where her literal communication style was appreciated rather than criticized. Where stimming was understood rather than mocked.

But the relief of unmasking online made masking at school feel even more unbearable by contrast.

One day at lunch, Emma zoned out again while Sarah was talking. But this time, instead of apologizing and forcing herself to focus, she just stayed quiet.

"Emma, seriously, what's going on with you?" Sarah asked, frustrated. "You've been so weird lately."

Something in Emma snapped. She was tired—so tired—of performing normalcy for people who didn't even try to understand her experience.

"I'm autistic," she said quietly.

The table went silent. Her friends exchanged glances.

"Wait, really?" Maya asked. "But you don't act autistic."

There it was. The comment Emma had been dreading, the reason she'd hidden her diagnosis for so long.

"Actually, I do," Emma said, surprised by the steadiness in her voice. "You just don't know what autism actually looks like because you're used to stereotypes. I mask constantly around you guys. I force myself to make eye contact even though it's uncomfortable. I pretend to care about conversations that bore me. I suppress my stims and sensory discomfort because I don't want you to think I'm weird."

Her friends stared at her.

"But you seem so normal," Jenna said.

"That's the point," Emma replied. "That's what masking is. I've been acting 'normal' for years, and it's burning me out. I'm exhausted all the time because I'm spending all my energy pretending to be someone I'm not."

"Why didn't you tell us?" Sarah asked, looking hurt.

"Because I was afraid you'd treat me differently. That you'd think I was less capable, or that I was using autism as an excuse, or that I'd become the 'autistic friend' instead of just Emma."

"We wouldn't have done that," Maya said, but her tone was uncertain.

"Maybe not intentionally," Emma said. "But people change how they act around you when they know you're disabled. They talk to you differently. They make assumptions about what you can and can't do."

The conversation was uncomfortable, but it was also honest in a way Emma's interactions with her friends had never been before. For once, she wasn't performing—she was just being real.

THE AFTERMATH WAS COMPLICATED. Some of Emma's friends made an effort to understand, asking questions and learning about autism from actually autistic sources instead of movies and stereotypes. Others gradually drifted away, uncomfortable with Emma's newfound directness and unwillingness to mask constantly.

It hurt to lose friends, but Emma also discovered that the relationships that survived her unmasking became deeper and more genuine. Maya started researching sensory sensitivities and began suggesting quieter hangout spots. Sarah stopped expecting Emma to participate in gossip she didn't care about.

More importantly, Emma found her people. Through Luna, she connected with a local neurodivergent teens group that met monthly. Walking into that first meeting and seeing other teenagers stimming, info-dumping about their special interests, and communicating in wonderfully direct ways felt like coming home.

"It's so nice to not have to explain everything," Emma told her mom after the meeting. "They just get it."

Her mom, who had spent years encouraging Emma to "work on her social skills," looked thoughtful. "I think I've been asking you to do something really hard without understanding the cost," she said. "I'm sorry."

"It's okay," Emma said. "You didn't know. But I need you to understand that I can't mask all the time anymore. It's not sustainable."

They talked for hours that night about what sustainable unmasking might look like. About accommodations Emma needed at school. About building her life in ways that worked with her neurodivergence rather than against it.

Emma still masked sometimes—in certain classes, during job interviews, around extended family. But she was learning to choose when to mask rather than defaulting to constant performance. She was learning to recognize the signs of burnout before she crashed completely. She was building a life that had room for both her masked self and her authentic self.

And most importantly, she was learning that the people worth keeping in her life were the ones who appreciated her unmasked self just as much—maybe even more—than the carefully constructed performance she'd spent years perfecting.

REFLECT

1. **Do you mask your neurodivergent traits? What does masking look like for you?**

Think about the behaviors, expressions, or responses you perform to appear more "normal" or neurotypical. This might include forcing eye contact, suppressing stims, pretending to follow conversations you don't understand, or hiding sensory discomfort.

____

____

____

____

____

2. **What environments or relationships allow you to unmask, even partially?**

Emma found her gaming community. Where do you feel safe being your authentic self? If you don't have any spaces like this yet, what might they look like?

____

____

____

____

____

3. What does masking cost you?

Consider the physical, emotional, and mental energy you spend on masking. How does it affect your mood, energy levels, relationships, or sense of self?

____

____

____

____

____

4. How do you think your relationships might change if you unmasked more? What fears come up?

Be honest about your concerns. The fear of rejection, judgment, or changed relationships is valid. But also consider: might some relationships actually improve with more authenticity?

____

____

____

____

____

5. What would you need in order to unmask more safely?

Think about supports, accommodations, or changes that would

make unmasking feel less risky. This might include finding your community, educating the people around you, or having backup plans for when unmasking doesn't go well.

____

____

____

____

____

~

ACT

This week, choose one space or situation where you'll experiment with unmasking, even in a small way.

This could look like:

- Stimming visibly in one environment where you usually suppress it
- Being direct in your communication instead of adding extra social niceties
- Declining an activity that's sensory overwhelming instead of forcing yourself to participate
- Telling one person about your neurodivergence
- Joining an online neurodivergent community
- Not forcing eye contact in a conversation
- Info-dumping about your special interest without apologizing

Start small. Pick something that feels manageable and relatively safe. Notice how it feels to unmask, even partially. Pay attention to what happens—both the relief you might experience and how others respond.

Document your experience:

- What did you choose to unmask?

- How did it feel?
- How did others respond?
- What did you learn about yourself or your relationships?
- Would you do it again?

Remember: Masking serves a protective function, and there's no shame in choosing to mask in situations where it genuinely keeps you safe. This exercise isn't about forcing yourself to unmask everywhere all at once. It's about experimenting with authenticity in one small, safer space and noticing what you discover.

2

DIFFERENT TIMELINE

Marcus stared at the group photo his friends had just posted: five of them crowded into Tyler's new car, all holding their driver's licenses and grinning at the camera. The caption read: *Freedom squad finally complete!* 🚗

Except the squad wasn't complete. Marcus wasn't in the photo because Marcus still didn't have his license. At seventeen, he was the only one in his friend group who hadn't passed the driving test. Most of them had gotten their licenses within weeks of turning sixteen. Marcus had failed the test three times.

It wasn't that he couldn't drive. He'd completed driver's ed and logged all his practice hours. But the actual test—with its time pressure, multiple simultaneous demands on his attention, and the stress of being evaluated—completely overwhelmed his ADHD brain. He'd forget to check his mirrors at the right moment, or he'd hyperfocus on one aspect of driving while missing another, or his anxiety would spike and he'd make a stupid mistake.

Each failure felt like proof that he was behind, that everyone else was moving forward while he stayed stuck.

Marcus's phone buzzed with another notification. The group chat was blowing up:

Tyler: Road trip to the beach this weekend! Who's in?
Jake: I'm down! Can drive
Sarah: Same!
Devon: Parents are lending me their car, I can take 4 people
Marcus typed and deleted three different responses before finally settling on: *Have fun! Can't make it this weekend.*

The truth was, he could make it. He just couldn't drive himself, and asking one of his friends to pick him up felt embarrassing. They'd all probably assume he couldn't go because of some family obligation, not because he was still dependent on his parents or older brother for transportation.

"How'd the test go?" his mom asked, poking her head into his room.

Marcus had been so absorbed in his phone that he'd forgotten she was waiting to hear. He'd taken the driving test that morning—his fourth attempt.

"Failed again," he said, trying to keep his voice neutral. "Apparently I didn't fully stop at a stop sign. I thought I did, but the examiner said I was still rolling."

His mom's face fell with sympathy that made Marcus feel worse. "Oh honey, I'm sorry. Do you want to schedule another test?"

"What's the point?" Marcus said, frustration spilling over. "Everyone else passed on their first or second try. I've failed four times. Maybe I'm just not meant to drive."

"That's not true. Your brain just processes things differently—"

"Yeah, differently as in worse," Marcus interrupted. "Can we not do the 'everyone's brain is special' speech right now? I know you're trying to help, but it doesn't change the fact that I'm seventeen and still can't do something literal teenagers can do."

His mom was quiet for a moment. "Your cousin Daniel called yesterday. He wanted to talk to you about something. Should I give him your number?"

Marcus shrugged. "Sure, whatever."

.   .   .

DANIEL CALLED THAT EVENING. He was Marcus's older cousin—twenty-four now, working as a software developer in Seattle. They'd been close when Marcus was younger, but had drifted apart as Daniel went to college and started his adult life.

"Your mom said you're having a rough time," Daniel said after the initial pleasantries.

"She told you about the driving test?" Marcus asked, embarrassed.

"She mentioned it. But I actually wanted to talk to you about something else. About timelines."

"Timelines?"

"Yeah. See, I also have ADHD. Your mom probably told you that."

Marcus vaguely remembered hearing that Daniel had been diagnosed in college, but they'd never really talked about it.

"I didn't know you knew," Marcus said.

"I only got diagnosed at twenty," Daniel continued. "Spent my whole childhood thinking I was lazy and unmotivated because I couldn't do things when everyone else could. I failed my driving test twice, didn't get my license until I was eighteen. Took me six years to finish my four-year degree. Got fired from my first two jobs because I couldn't manage the deadlines and organization they required."

"That sounds rough," Marcus said, not sure where this was going.

"It was. But here's the thing I wish someone had told me back then: not everyone is on the same timeline, and that's okay. The way school and society are set up, there's this idea that everyone should hit the same milestones at the same age. Driver's license at sixteen. High school graduation at eighteen. College degree at twenty-two. First real job by twenty-three."

"Yeah, that's basically what everyone expects."

"Right. But those timelines were created by and for neurotypical people. They don't account for brains that work differently, or for people who need different types of support, or for the reality that some of us need more time to develop certain skills."

Marcus felt something shift in his chest. He'd never thought about it that way before.

"I got my license later than my friends," Daniel continued. "Graduated college later. Started my career later. But you know what? I still got there. And the extra time I took actually helped me figure out systems and strategies that work for my ADHD brain. Now I'm successful in my field, making good money, doing work I love. The fact that I took longer to get here doesn't matter at all."

"But don't you feel like you wasted time?" Marcus asked.

"No. I feel like I took the time I needed. There's a difference." Daniel paused. "Look, I'm not saying it doesn't suck to watch your friends hit milestones before you do. That FOMO is real. But beating yourself up for not matching their timeline just makes it worse."

"So what am I supposed to do? Just accept that I'm always going to be behind?"

"You're not behind," Daniel said firmly. "You're on a different path. Some of the most successful people I know—especially neurodivergent people—took non-traditional routes. They didn't follow the standard timeline, and that's actually what made them successful. They figured out what worked for their brains instead of forcing themselves into a mold that was never designed for them."

THE CONVERSATION with Daniel stayed with Marcus over the following weeks. He started noticing how much of his stress came from comparing himself to his peers—not because he actually wanted the same things they wanted, but because society told him he should want those things on that timeline.

Take college, for example. Marcus's friends were all stressing about college applications, SAT scores, and acceptance letters. The assumption was that everyone would go to a four-year university immediately after high school. But when Marcus really thought about it, the idea of four more years of traditional classroom learning made him want to crawl out of his skin.

He'd always been more interested in hands-on, practical learning. He taught himself coding through online tutorials because he found them more engaging than textbooks. He'd built his own computer because he wanted to understand how the components worked together. But those interests didn't fit neatly into the college-prep curriculum his school emphasized.

One day, his school counselor called him in to discuss his post-graduation plans.

"Your grades are decent, Marcus, but you haven't started any college applications. Is there a reason for the delay?"

Marcus hesitated. "I'm not sure college is the right fit for me."

The counselor frowned. "You're certainly capable of college work. Is this about the cost? There are scholarships and financial aid—"

"It's not about money," Marcus interrupted. "It's about whether sitting in lecture halls for four more years is actually going to help me do what I want to do."

"And what do you want to do?"

"Something with computers. IT, maybe, or software development. But I learn better by doing things, not by reading about them or listening to lectures."

The counselor pulled out some brochures. "Have you considered technical colleges? They offer shorter certification programs with more hands-on learning. It's not the traditional four-year path, but it might fit your learning style better."

Marcus took the brochures, surprised. He'd expected his counselor to push the university route harder.

"There's no shame in alternative paths," the counselor continued. "Some people's brains and interests align better with hands-on, practical learning. That doesn't make them less intelligent—it makes them differently intelligent."

THAT EVENING, Marcus sat down with his parents.

"I don't think I want to go to a traditional four-year university," he said, forcing the words out before he could second-guess himself.

His parents exchanged glances. "What do you mean?" his dad asked.

"I mean, I've been trying to force myself into the standard academic path, and it's not working. I'm stressed all the time, my grades are okay but not great, and I don't see how four more years of the same is going to help me."

"So what are you thinking instead?" his mom asked carefully.

Marcus pulled out the technical college brochures. "Programs like this. Shorter, more focused, more hands-on. I could get certified in computer repair or IT support, start working and making money, and then figure out if I want more education later."

"But you're smart enough for regular college," his dad said, and Marcus could hear the concern—the fear that Marcus was selling himself short.

"I know I'm smart," Marcus said. "But traditional college is designed for a certain type of learning, and that's not how my brain works best. This isn't me giving up—it's me choosing a path that actually fits me instead of trying to contort myself to fit a path that was designed for neurotypical people."

His parents were quiet, processing.

"What about your friends?" his mom asked. "Won't they all be going to four-year schools?"

"Probably. And yeah, that's hard. But I've been trying to follow their timeline, and all it's done is make me feel like a failure. I need to figure out my own timeline."

His parents looked at each other again, having one of those silent conversations that long-married couples can have.

"Okay," his dad said finally. "Let's look at these programs together and figure out what makes sense for you."

THREE MONTHS LATER, Marcus finally passed his driving test—his fifth attempt. When he got the news, his friends were appropriately congratulatory, but Marcus noticed they didn't quite understand why it meant so much to him.

"Dude, finally!" Tyler said, clapping him on the shoulder. "Now you can actually make road trips."

"Yeah," Marcus said, but what he was really celebrating wasn't just the license. It was the proof that he could achieve things even if it took him longer than everyone else. That his timeline was valid even when it didn't match up with his peers'.

That night, Daniel called to congratulate him.

"How does it feel?" he asked.

"Good," Marcus said. "Really good. Not just because I have the license, but because I proved to myself that I could do it even if it took longer."

"That's exactly the right attitude," Daniel said. "You know, a lot of people with ADHD end up being late bloomers. We take longer to develop executive function, longer to figure out what works for our brains, longer to find our paths. But that doesn't mean we don't get there."

"I'm starting to believe that," Marcus admitted.

"Good. Because here's something else I've learned: some of the most successful neurodivergent people I know took non-traditional paths. They weren't the ones who did everything 'on time' according to society's schedule. They were the ones who figured out what timeline worked for them and then committed to that timeline, even when other people didn't understand it."

As Marcus hung up, he thought about the future—not the future he'd been trying to force himself into, but the one he was actually building. It looked different from his friends' futures. It was on a different timeline.

And for the first time, that felt okay.

SENIOR YEAR CONTINUED, and Marcus watched his friends stress about college applications, SAT scores, and acceptance letters. He felt some FOMO, sure. But he also felt relief that he wasn't caught up in that particular race anymore.

He'd enrolled in dual enrollment classes at the technical college, taking IT fundamentals while finishing high school. The hands-on, practical approach to learning worked so much better for his brain than traditional lecture classes. His grades were good —not because he was forcing himself to focus, but because he was genuinely interested and the teaching style matched how he learned.

He'd also gotten a part-time job at a local computer repair shop. His boss, who also had ADHD, appreciated Marcus's ability to hyper-focus on troubleshooting problems and didn't mind when Marcus needed to take quick breaks to manage his attention.

By graduation, while his friends were heading off to universities across the state, Marcus had a full-time job offer from the repair shop and a plan to complete his IT certifications while working. It wasn't the path anyone had expected him to take, but it was working.

At the graduation party his parents threw, his uncle cornered him with the inevitable question: "So, what are your plans? What school are you going to?"

Before Marcus could answer, Daniel—who had flown in for the graduation—stepped in.

"Marcus is going to technical college and working in IT," Daniel said proudly. "He's actually ahead of where I was at his age. Took me two extra years to figure out what he's already figured out."

Marcus's uncle looked uncertain, clearly trying to figure out if this was good news or a polite way of describing failure.

"I'm on a different timeline," Marcus explained, using the language he'd learned from Daniel. "Not better or worse than anyone else's. Just different. And that's okay."

His uncle nodded slowly, still not quite getting it, but Marcus didn't need him to. Marcus had finally stopped measuring his life against everyone else's milestones.

He was on his own timeline now. And that was exactly where he needed to be.

REFLECT

1. **What milestones or achievements do you feel "behind" on compared to your peers?**

Be specific. Is it academic achievements, social milestones, life skills, independence markers? Write them down and acknowledge the feelings that come up.

____

____

____

____

____

2. Where did you learn that these things "should" happen at a certain age?

Think about the messages you've received from parents, teachers, friends, social media, or society in general about what you should be accomplishing and when.

____

____

____

____

____

3. Are these milestones actually important to you, or do you feel pressured to want them because everyone else is achieving them?

This is a tough question. Really consider whether you genuinely want these things, or whether you're pursuing them because you think you're supposed to.

____

____

____

____

____

4. What strengths or interests do you have that don't fit into traditional timelines?

Marcus was good at hands-on learning and computer work, but those didn't align with the college-prep timeline. What are you good at that might require a different path?

____

____

____

____

____

5. If you removed all comparison to others, what would your ideal timeline look like?

Let yourself dream here. If you truly didn't care what anyone else thought, how would you structure your education, career path, or life milestones?

____

____

____

____

____

∼

ACT

This week, give yourself explicit permission to be on your own timeline for three specific things.

Write them down in this format:

"I give myself permission to _________ [achieve this thing] on my own timeline. This might take me longer than my peers, and that's okay. My brain works differently, and I need different time and approaches to master certain skills."

For example:

- "I give myself permission to get my driver's license on my own timeline, even if it takes me five tries instead of one."

- "I give myself permission to figure out my career path on my own timeline, even if my friends all know what they want to do and I'm still exploring."
- "I give myself permission to develop executive function skills on my own timeline, even if I'm still working on basics that my peers mastered years ago."

After you write these three statements:

1. **Put them somewhere visible** (bathroom mirror, phone wallpaper, notebook you use daily)
2. **Read them daily** for at least one week
3. **Notice when you compare yourself to others** on these three things, and consciously redirect your thoughts to your permission statements
4. **Find one person** (friend, family member, therapist, online community) and share your different timeline with them

Optional extension: Research one successful neurodivergent person who took a non-traditional path. Learn about their timeline and how they got to where they are now. Notice that "taking longer" or "doing things differently" didn't prevent their success—it often contributed to it.

3

—————

EXECUTIVE FUNCTION FAILS

Jayden stared at the text from Coach Martinez:

Need to see you after practice tomorrow. Important.

He knew what this was about. It was always about the same thing: his inability to show up on time, turn in paperwork, or remember the million small details that everyone else seemed to handle effortlessly.

This week alone, he'd been late to practice twice (once by five minutes, once by twenty), forgotten his permission slip for the away game, and completely missed the deadline for his history project that was now three days overdue. It wasn't that he didn't care. Basketball was the most important thing in Jayden's life. His history grade mattered because he needed to maintain eligibility for the team.

He just... couldn't seem to make his brain cooperate with basic organizational tasks.

"Just set more alarms," his teammates would say, like he hadn't already tried that. He had seven alarms on his phone. He snoozed through all of them because his brain didn't register their urgency until it was too late.

"Just write things down," his teachers suggested, like he hadn't tried every planner, app, and organizational system known to humanity. He'd write things down and then completely forget to check what he'd written.

"Just try harder," everyone said, like effort was the issue. Like he wasn't already trying as hard as he could.

Jayden had been diagnosed with ADHD in elementary school, but he'd never really understood what that meant beyond "takes medication and has trouble paying attention." Now, at fifteen, he was starting to realize that his executive function challenges—time management, organization, task initiation, working memory— weren't going to magically disappear just because he tried really, really hard.

THE NEXT DAY, Jayden showed up to practice exactly on time. He'd set twelve alarms, put reminders on three different devices, and asked his mom to physically drive him to make sure he arrived when he was supposed to.

Coach Martinez noticed. "On time today, Jayden. That's good."

After practice, Coach called him over. Jayden's stomach twisted with anxiety.

"Have a seat," Coach said, gesturing to the bench. His tone was serious but not angry.

"I know I've been messing up a lot," Jayden started. "But I'm trying, Coach. I really am."

"I know you're trying," Coach said. "That's not what concerns me. What concerns me is that trying harder doesn't seem to be working."

Jayden felt heat rise to his face. "I have ADHD. I'm on medication. I don't know what else to do."

"I know about your ADHD," Coach said. "What I'm wondering is whether you actually understand what that means and what kind of support you need."

"What do you mean?"

Coach leaned back. "I had a conversation with the athletic director and your school counselor. We're not trying to kick you off the team, Jayden. But we are concerned that you're struggling and we don't know how to help you."

"I just need to be better about being on time and remembering things," Jayden said automatically.

"See, that's what worries me. You're talking about this like it's a willpower problem. Like you just need to want it more or try harder. But executive function doesn't work that way."

Jayden blinked. He'd never heard a coach talk about executive function before.

"I've been reading about ADHD," Coach continued. "Especially about how it affects athletes. Did you know that executive function challenges aren't about effort or intelligence? They're about how your brain processes time, prioritizes tasks, and manages multiple demands."

"I guess I knew that theoretically," Jayden admitted. "But I still feel like if I just tried harder—"

"That's the trap," Coach interrupted. "Trying harder at strategies that don't work for your brain is just going to burn you out. What you need is to build systems that actually accommodate how your brain works."

"Like what?"

"That's what we're going to figure out. But first, I need you to stop treating your executive function challenges like personal failures. They're neurological differences. You don't shame someone for needing glasses to see, right?"

Jayden had never thought about it that way.

"Here's what I'm proposing," Coach said. "The assistant coach, Rodriguez, also has ADHD. He's offered to mentor you on building systems that work. You'll meet with him twice a week for the next month to develop strategies specifically for time management and organization. If we see improvement—not perfection, but real improvement—you stay on the team."

"And if there's no improvement?"

"Then we'll reevaluate. But Jayden, I'm not expecting you to magically become neurotypical. I'm expecting you to learn strategies that work with your ADHD brain instead of fighting against it."

THE NEXT DAY, Jayden met Coach Rodriguez in his office. Rodriguez was in his late twenties, energetic and direct in a way that made Jayden comfortable immediately.

"So, Coach Martinez tells me you're drowning in executive function fails," Rodriguez said, getting straight to the point.

"Pretty much," Jayden admitted.

"Okay, let's start with the most pressing issue. What's threatening your eligibility right now?"

"Being late to practice. Missing assignments. Forgetting paperwork."

"Alright. Let's break those down one at a time. Start with lateness. Walk me through what happens on days when you're late."

Jayden thought back. "Usually I'm doing something else—playing video games, or on my phone, or talking to someone—and I just lose track of time. Then suddenly I realize I have to leave and I'm not ready yet. I'm searching for my practice clothes or my shoes or my water bottle. By the time I actually leave, I'm already late."

"Classic time blindness," Rodriguez said. "Your brain doesn't naturally track time passing. It's either 'now' or 'not now,' right?"

"Exactly! It's like time doesn't exist until suddenly it's urgent and I'm in a panic."

"Okay, so 'just set an alarm' doesn't work because—"

"Because my brain hears the alarm but doesn't register it as urgent until it's too late," Jayden finished.

"Right. So we need a system that works with your time blindness, not against it. Here's what I do." Rodriguez pulled out his phone. "I don't set one alarm. I set a sequence of alarms with very specific labels."

He showed Jayden his screen:

- 3:00 PM - "Basketball in 90 minutes - START GETTING READY"
- 3:30 PM - "Basketball in 60 minutes - Pack your bag NOW"
- 4:00 PM - "Basketball in 30 minutes - Leave in 10 minutes"
- 4:10 PM - "Basketball in 20 minutes - LEAVE NOW"
- 4:20 PM - "Basketball in 10 minutes - You should be driving"

"That's... a lot of alarms," Jayden said.

"Yep. But here's the thing—my brain needs external time markers because it can't generate them internally. These alarms aren't annoying reminders. They're accommodations. They're my external executive function."

"And this works for you?"

"Most of the time. When it doesn't, it's usually because I ignored the 3:00 PM alarm and then suddenly the 4:20 alarm is going off and I'm still not ready. But even then, I leave right away instead of being twenty minutes late."

Jayden pulled out his phone. "Okay, help me set these up for practice."

They spent twenty minutes creating alarm sequences for practice, games, and the morning routine before school. Rodriguez insisted on specific, action-oriented labels for each alarm.

"Your brain needs to know exactly what action to take," Rodriguez explained. "Not just 'practice soon' but 'pack your bag NOW.' Make the command so specific that your brain can't argue with it."

NEXT, they tackled the forgotten items problem.

"I always forget something," Jayden said. "My uniform, my water bottle, my permission slips. It's like my brain can't hold onto a mental checklist."

"Because it probably can't," Rodriguez said. "Working memory challenges are real. So we make the checklist external."

He pulled out a laminated card from his gym bag. On it was a simple checklist:

BASKETBALL PRACTICE ▫ Uniform (jersey, shorts, socks) ▫ Shoes ▫ Water bottle ▫ Phone & headphones ▫ Homework (if staying after) ▫ Permission slips (check phone for alerts)

"I literally check this off every single time I pack my bag," Rodriguez said. "Even though I've been doing this for years and I know what I need. Because my working memory is unreliable."

"Doesn't that feel kind of... childish?" Jayden asked.

"Does a pilot feel childish for using a pre-flight checklist?" Rodriguez countered. "They're literal experts who've flown hundreds of times, but they still use checklists because human memory is fallible. Why should you hold yourself to a higher standard than trained pilots?"

That perspective shift hit Jayden hard. He'd been treating accommodations like embarrassing crutches when they were really just practical tools.

They created checklists for Jayden's basketball bag, his school backpack, and his morning routine. Rodriguez showed him how to attach them to the relevant bags with carabiners so they were always accessible.

"The key is making these systems harder to forget than the actual items," Rodriguez said. "Put the checklist where you literally can't miss it."

THE HOMEWORK and deadline problem was trickier.

"I write assignments down," Jayden explained. "But then I forget to check my planner. Or I check it but I don't process that something is due soon. Or I see it's due in a week and my brain interprets that as 'forever from now' and I put it off until it's suddenly due tomorrow."

"Ah, the 'now' or 'not now' problem again," Rodriguez said. "Your brain doesn't process future deadlines as real until they're immediate."

"Exactly. And then teachers say I procrastinate, but it's not that I choose to wait. It's like my brain literally cannot engage with the task until there's urgency."

"That's actually a real thing—ADHD brains often need deadline pressure to activate the executive function required for task initiation. The problem is, waiting until the last minute creates stress and usually means the work is rushed."

"So what do I do?"

"You create artificial urgency earlier," Rodriguez said. "We trick your brain into thinking the deadline is sooner than it actually is."

He showed Jayden his system: every assignment went into his phone calendar not on the actual due date, but three days before. His brain experienced the urgency three days early, giving him time to actually complete the work.

"But what if my brain figures out that the fake deadline isn't real?" Jayden asked.

"Then you adjust. Some people need fake deadlines to be one day early, some need a week. You experiment until you find what works for your brain."

They also set up body doubling sessions—Rodriguez explained that many ADHD brains work better with someone else present, even if that person isn't directly helping.

"Twice a week, you and I are going to have homework time," Rodriguez said. "You bring your work, I bring mine, we sit in the same room and work on our separate stuff. Your brain will find it easier to focus when there's another person there maintaining focus."

OVER THE NEXT MONTH, Jayden implemented his new systems. It wasn't perfect. He still missed some alarms, still forgot things occasionally, still had moments of time blindness. But the difference was dramatic.

He was late to practice only once (by five minutes, and he texted ahead to let Coach know). He turned in his assignments on time—

not perfect assignments, but completed ones. He remembered his permission slips because they were literally on a checklist he couldn't pack his bag without seeing.

More importantly, Jayden stopped beating himself up every time something went wrong. When he forgot his water bottle one day, instead of spiraling into self-criticism, he just thought, "Okay, the checklist system didn't work this time. What adjustment do I need to make?"

"You seem different," his teammate Carlos commented one day. "Like, less stressed."

"I'm working with Coach Rodriguez on systems for my ADHD," Jayden explained. "It's actually helping."

"That's cool that the coaches are helping with that," Carlos said. "My brother has ADHD too and he struggles with the same stuff."

Jayden pulled out his laminated checklist. "You want to take a picture? These have been game-changers for me."

As Carlos snapped a photo, Jayden realized something important: he wasn't ashamed of his accommodations anymore. They weren't signs of weakness—they were signs of self-awareness and problem-solving.

AT THE END of the month, Coach Martinez called Jayden in again.

"So, update me on how things are going," Coach said.

"Better," Jayden said. "Not perfect, but way better. I've been using the alarm sequences, the checklists, the fake deadlines. And I've been doing body doubling with Coach Rodriguez twice a week for homework."

"I've noticed the improvement," Coach said. "You've been on time or early to every practice but one. Your teachers report that your missing assignments are way down. That's significant progress."

"Thanks. I feel less like I'm drowning all the time."

"Good. So here's what I want you to understand: these systems you've built? They're not temporary training wheels until your brain gets better. They're permanent accommodations for how your brain works."

"I know," Jayden said. "Coach Rodriguez explained that."

"Because I see a lot of ADHD students who develop good systems and then abandon them once things improve. They think, 'I'm doing better now, I don't need these anymore.' But the reason they're doing better is *because* of the systems."

"That makes sense."

"You're going to need accommodations for the rest of your life, Jayden. That doesn't mean you're broken. It means you're working with your neurodivergence instead of against it. That's actually a sign of maturity and self-awareness."

Jayden felt something release in his chest—a tension he'd been carrying for years. The belief that he should eventually be able to function without support, that needing accommodations meant he was failing.

"So I'm good with the team?" he asked.

"You're good with the team," Coach confirmed. "And I'm impressed with how seriously you've taken this. A lot of people would have just tried harder at the same strategies that weren't working. You actually changed your approach."

THAT NIGHT, Jayden's mom noticed him setting up his alarms for the next day.

"Those certainly are a lot of alarms," she commented, watching him program the sequence.

"Yeah, I need them," Jayden said simply. "My brain doesn't track time naturally, so the alarms are my external time awareness."

"Does it bother you? Having to set all these up?"

Jayden thought about it. "Sometimes I wish I could just naturally remember things and be on time like everyone else. But I can't. So I either accept my brain and build systems that work, or I keep failing and feeling terrible about myself. The systems are way better."

His mom smiled. "I'm proud of you for figuring that out. A lot of adults haven't learned that lesson yet."

"Coach Rodriguez helped. He has ADHD too, and he's really successful. Seeing him use all these same strategies made me realize it's not about outgrowing ADHD or becoming 'normal.' It's about building a life that works with my brain instead of against it."

"That's very wise."

"Also," Jayden added, "I'm not going to feel bad about needing accommodations anymore. Pilots use checklists and nobody thinks they're incompetent. Why should I hold myself to a different standard?"

His mom laughed. "Did Coach Rodriguez use that analogy?"

"He did. And it really helped."

THE REST of the season went well. Jayden didn't become perfect—no one is. He still had executive function challenges, still struggled with tasks that required sustained organization and time management. But he had strategies now. He had systems. He had self-awareness about how his brain worked and what he needed to accommodate it.

More importantly, he'd stopped treating his ADHD as a character flaw to overcome and started treating it as a neurological difference to accommodate. That shift in perspective changed everything.

Near the end of the season, a freshman named Tyler approached him after practice.

"Hey, I heard you work with Coach Rodriguez on ADHD stuff," Tyler said hesitantly. "I just got diagnosed and I'm struggling with the same things you were. Do you think... could you show me some of the systems you use?"

Jayden felt a surge of unexpected pride. Six months ago, he'd been ashamed of his struggles, hiding his difficulties and pretending he didn't need help. Now he was someone who could help others navigate the same challenges.

"Yeah, definitely," Jayden said. "Let me show you my alarm

sequences and checklists. And I'll introduce you to Coach Rodriguez —he's the one who taught me all this stuff."

As he walked Tyler through the systems that had changed his life, Jayden realized something important: his executive function challenges would never go away. But with the right supports, they didn't have to define him or limit him.

He could thrive with ADHD. He just needed to work with his brain, not against it.

~

REFLECT

1. What executive function challenges impact your daily life the most?

Executive function includes: time management, organization, task initiation, working memory, planning, prioritization, impulse control, and emotional regulation. Which of these areas cause you the most difficulty?

____

____

____

____

____

2. What strategies have you tried that didn't work? Why do you think they failed?

Think about the well-meaning advice you've received: "just set an alarm," "just write it down," "just try harder." Why didn't these standard strategies work for your ADHD brain?

____

____

____

____

____

. . .

3. Do you treat your executive function challenges as character flaws or neurological differences?

Be honest: when you forget something or run late, do you think "I'm so lazy/stupid/irresponsible" or do you think "my working memory/time blindness is a challenge that needs accommodation"?

____

____

____

____

____

4. What accommodations or supports do you already use? Do you feel ashamed of them or proud of them?

List the tools, systems, or supports you currently have in place. Then examine your feelings about them. Are you hiding these accommodations, or are you open about needing them?

____

____

____

____

____

5. If you removed all judgment and comparison to neurotypical people, what systems or accommodations would you want to try?

Without worrying about what's "normal" or what others might think, what supports would actually help you function better?

____

____

____

____

____

∼

ACT

This week, choose ONE executive function challenge and build a system to accommodate it—not to eliminate it, but to work with it.

Use these steps:

Step 1: Identify the specific challenge Not "I'm bad at time management," but "I lose track of time when I'm doing something engaging and then I'm late to commitments."

Step 2: Understand why standard solutions don't work for your brain Example: "Simple alarms don't work because my brain hears them but doesn't process them as urgent until it's too late."

Step 3: Design an accommodation that works WITH your brain Example: Alarm sequences with specific action commands, not just time reminders.

Step 4: Build the system Actually create the tool, checklist, alarm sequence, or structure you need. Make it easy to access and hard to forget.

Step 5: Test and adjust Use the system for a full week. Notice what works and what doesn't. Adjust as needed—this is iterative, not perfect.

Specific system ideas to try:

For time blindness:

- Alarm sequences with specific action commands (like Jayden and Coach Rodriguez)
- Visual timers that show time passing
- Calendar notifications at multiple intervals before events

For forgetting items:

- Laminated checklists attached to relevant bags
- Taking photos of what you need before leaving
- "Launch pad" by your door with everything you need

For starting tasks:

- Fake deadlines set 2-3 days before actual deadlines
- Body doubling (working alongside someone else)
- Breaking tasks into 5-minute chunks instead of full projects

For working memory challenges:

- Immediate capture system (voice notes, quick phone entries)
- Visual reminders in places you'll definitely see them
- Color-coding or symbol systems that make information easier to process

For organization:

- One place for everything (not "organized" but "always in the same spot")
- Fewer organizational systems (more is not better for ADHD brains)
- Clear bins/containers where you can see contents

Important mindset shifts to practice:

- "This isn't cheating—it's accommodation"
- "Pilots use checklists; I can too"
- "Working with my brain, not against it"
- "Progress, not perfection"

Document your experience:

- What challenge did you address?
- What system did you create?
- Did it work? Why or why not?

- What adjustments do you need to make?
- How did it feel to use accommodations unapologetically?

Remember: You're not trying to become neurotypical. You're building systems that let your neurodivergent brain function at its best.

4

SENSORY OVERLOAD

Kai stared at the group chat, watching the excitement build:

Mia: GUYS! I got tickets to see The Violet Storm! November 15th!

James: NO WAY! That's going to be AMAZING

Priya: I'm so in! How many tickets?

Mia: Six! So all of us can go! Kai, you're coming right?

Kai's stomach dropped. A concert. A crowded, loud, overwhelming concert at a venue he'd never been to before, with flashing lights and screaming fans and unpredictable chaos.

His fingers hovered over the keyboard. He wanted to say yes. He loved his friends. He even liked The Violet Storm's music. But the thought of being in that environment for hours made his skin crawl and his anxiety spike.

Kai: Sounds fun! Let me check with my parents

It was a lie. Well, a delay tactic. He'd check with his parents, they'd say yes because they always encouraged him to "get out more and be social," and then he'd be trapped into going to something that would be sensory hell.

Kai was autistic, and while he'd gotten better at managing his sensory sensitivities over the years, concerts were still firmly in the "absolutely not" category. Too loud. Too crowded. Too much unpredictability. Too many strangers in his personal space.

But how could he explain that to his friends without sounding weird or dramatic? They'd been to concerts before and loved them. To them, it was just fun. They wouldn't understand why the same experience that energized them would completely overwhelm him.

Over the next two weeks, the group chat exploded with concert planning. What to wear, when to meet up, whether to get there early for merch. Kai participated minimally, hoping maybe if he just didn't talk about it, everyone would forget he'd sort of agreed to go.

No such luck.

"So are you coming Friday?" Mia asked at lunch, exactly one week before the concert.

"I'm not sure yet," Kai hedged.

"Dude, you have to come," James said. "It's going to be legendary. The Violet Storm never comes to our city."

"Plus we already have your ticket," Priya added. "Mia bought all six together."

Guilt joined the anxiety in Kai's stomach. Mia had spent her money on a ticket for him. He couldn't just not show up now.

"I'll be there," Kai heard himself say.

His friends cheered. Kai felt like he was agreeing to walk into a fire.

The week before the concert, Kai couldn't sleep. He kept imagining the venue—the crowds pressing in from all sides, the music so loud he'd feel it in his chest, the strobe lights that would make his eyes hurt, the unpredictable screaming and movement of thousands of people.

His mom noticed him picking at his breakfast Thursday morning.

"What's wrong?" she asked.

"Nothing."

"Kai."

He sighed. "There's this concert tomorrow. My friends are all going."

"That sounds fun! You like The Violet Storm."

"I like their music on Spotify, in my room, at a volume I control," Kai clarified. "I don't like crowds and loud noise and chaos."

His mom's expression shifted to understanding. She knew about his sensory issues—they'd been dealing with them since he was little. "Did you tell your friends you're not comfortable with concerts?"

"No."

"Why not?"

"Because they'll think I'm weird. Or making a big deal out of nothing. Or being antisocial."

"Or they might understand and want to help you feel comfortable," his mom suggested.

Kai shook his head. "They won't get it. Neurotypical people never understand sensory stuff. They just think you're being dramatic or picky."

"Some people are like that," his mom agreed. "But good friends—real friends—care about your wellbeing. And these seem like good friends."

"They are," Kai admitted. "That's why I don't want to be the problem friend who can't do normal fun things."

His mom was quiet for a moment. "Kai, you're not a problem. You have different sensory needs than your friends. That's not a character flaw. And if they can't understand that, then maybe they're not as good friends as you think they are."

THAT NIGHT, Kai lay in bed with his noise-canceling headphones on, trying to regulate the anxiety that was making his whole body feel electric and wrong. He pulled up the group chat and started typing several times, but he couldn't find the right words.

How do you explain sensory overload to people who've never experienced it? How do you make them understand that what's "just loud" to them is actually physically painful to you? That what's "just crowded" to them triggers a fight-or-flight response in you?

Finally, at 11 PM, he gave up on sleep and texted Mia privately:

Kai: Hey, can I talk to you about something?

Mia: Of course! What's up?

Kai: About the concert tomorrow

Mia: You're still coming right? Please don't bail, it won't be the same without you

Kai took a breath and forced himself to be honest:

Kai: I want to come because I care about you guys and I don't want to miss out. But I need you to know something. I'm autistic (you probably knew that already) and I have pretty significant sensory sensitivities. Concerts are really overwhelming for me—the noise, the crowds, the lights. I'm kind of dreading it even though I want to hang out with everyone.

He hit send before he could delete it again, then immediately regretted it. What if she thought he was being dramatic? What if she was annoyed that he was making things complicated?

Mia: Oh wow, I had no idea concerts were hard for you! I knew you were autistic but I didn't really know what that meant for sensory stuff. Thank you for telling me.

Kai: I probably should have said something sooner

Mia: Why didn't you?

Kai: Because I didn't want to be the weird kid who can't handle normal things

Mia: Kai, you're not weird. You just experience things differently. Can you help me understand what specifically is overwhelming about concerts?

The relief of being asked—of not having to prove or justify or defend—made Kai's eyes sting.

Kai: The volume is physically painful, not just loud. The crowd pressing in makes me feel trapped and panicky. Flashing lights hurt my eyes and make it hard to process what's happening. The unpredictability of when people will scream or surge forward keeps me in constant high alert. By the end, I'm usually completely shutdown—can't talk, can't think, sometimes can't even get myself home safely.

Mia: That sounds really hard

Kai: It is. But I don't want to miss out on stuff with you guys

Mia: Okay, let me think. Is there anything that would make concerts more manageable for you?

Kai blinked. He'd expected sympathy at best, maybe annoyance at worst. He hadn't expected problem-solving.

Kai: I've never really thought about it because I always just avoid concerts completely

Mia: Well, let's think about it now. What if we could address some of those sensory issues?

THE NEXT MORNING, Mia called an emergency video chat with the whole friend group.

"Okay, so change of plans for tonight," she announced. "Kai helped me understand that concerts can be really overwhelming for autistic people because of sensory stuff—loud noise, crowds, lights. So we're going to make some adjustments so everyone can actually enjoy this."

Kai felt his face heat up. He hadn't expected Mia to tell everyone.

"What kind of adjustments?" James asked.

"Well, first, Kai's going to wear his noise-reducing earplugs—"

"I have earplugs?" Kai interrupted.

"You do now. I researched them last night. There are special ones designed for concerts that reduce volume without making everything muffled. I ordered them for express delivery and they should arrive at your house this afternoon."

Kai was speechless.

"Second," Mia continued, "we're not going to try to get right up front near the stage. We're going to stay toward the back where there's more space and it's slightly less loud."

"But the best view is up front," James protested.

"The best view for *you* is up front," Priya corrected him. "The best experience for Kai is where he can actually be comfortable enough to enjoy the music."

"Oh. Yeah, that makes sense."

"Third," Mia said, "we're going to have an exit strategy. Kai, if it gets too overwhelming, you text the group chat 'red light' and we all leave together. No questions, no guilt trip, we just go. Deal?"

"You guys would leave early?" Kai asked, stunned.

"Dude, we're there to hang out together," James said. "If you're having a miserable time, that defeats the whole purpose."

"Also," Priya added, "I did some research too. The venue has a sensory-friendly viewing area. It's off to the side, slightly elevated, with less crowd density and the option to step into a quiet room if you need a break. I called and got us access."

"You did research?" Kai repeated, feeling something crack open in his chest.

"Of course we did," Mia said. "You're our friend. We want you there, and we want you to actually have a good time, not just suffer through it to make us happy."

THAT AFTERNOON, the earplugs arrived. Kai tried them on and was amazed—they reduced the volume significantly without making everything sound muffled or distorted. He could still hear music clearly; it was just at a level that didn't hurt.

He texted Mia: *Thank you for the earplugs. And for... everything.*

Mia: Of course! Are you feeling better about tonight?

Kai: Yeah. I'm still nervous but not dreading it anymore

Mia: Good. And remember, if it's too much, we leave. No shame in that.

THE CONCERT WAS STILL OVERWHELMING, but it was manageable. The sensory-friendly viewing area made a huge difference—there was space to move, the volume was slightly lower, and knowing he could step into the quiet room if needed reduced his anxiety significantly.

Halfway through, Kai did need a break. The cumulative sensory input was building up, and he could feel himself starting to get overstimulated. He stepped into the quiet room, which was dimly lit and nearly silent, and sat on a cushioned bench with his eyes closed for ten minutes.

Priya came to check on him.

"You okay?" she asked quietly.

"Yeah, just needed a break from the stimulation."

"That's smart. Can I sit with you for a bit? It's actually kind of nice in here."

They sat in comfortable silence for a few minutes. Kai's nervous system began to settle, the overwhelming sensation fading from unbearable to merely intense.

"Thanks for not making me feel weird about this," Kai said.

"Why would we make you feel weird? You're taking care of yourself. That's healthy."

"A lot of people would think I'm being dramatic or overly sensitive."

Priya shook her head. "Those people are wrong. Sensory stuff is real. My little cousin has autism and she has major sensory issues with food textures. I've seen her literally throw up from eating something with the wrong texture. It's not dramatic—it's just how her nervous system works."

"I wish more people understood that."

"Me too. But you know what? You're helping us understand. Before this, I just thought autism meant you were really good at math or whatever." She laughed at herself. "I know that sounds ignorant now. But you trusting us enough to explain what you actually experience—that's helping us be better friends and better people."

THEY WENT BACK out for the last part of the concert. Kai wore his earplugs, stood at the back of the sensory-friendly area where he had space, and actually enjoyed himself. The music was good. His friends were there. He wasn't suffering.

When the concert ended, James turned to him. "So? Was it as bad as you thought it would be?"

"Actually, no," Kai admitted. "It was still a lot of sensory input, and

I'm definitely going to need to recover tomorrow. But with the accommodations, it was manageable. Even kind of fun."

"Good," Mia said, throwing her arm around his shoulders briefly before remembering he didn't love unexpected touch and pulling back. "Because you're part of this group and we want you at stuff."

"Even if it means making accommodations?"

"Especially if it means making accommodations," Priya said firmly. "That's what friends do."

On the drive home, Kai's dad picked him up and immediately noticed the earplugs.

"How'd it go?" he asked.

"Better than I expected," Kai said. "My friends made a lot of accommodations so I could actually enjoy it instead of just endure it."

"That's great. I'm glad they were understanding."

"Me too. I think I spent so much time assuming people wouldn't get it that I didn't give them a chance to try."

His dad smiled. "That's a pretty mature realization."

When Kai got home, he was exhausted in the specific way that came after sensory overload—drained, slightly shaky, needing quiet and darkness and minimal stimulation. But he wasn't shutdown. He wasn't in pain. He wasn't traumatized.

He'd actually had a good time.

The next day, he woke up to a group chat message from Mia:

Mia: Okay so I've been thinking. If we're going to keep including Kai in group activities (which obviously we are), we should probably learn more about sensory stuff and autism in general. I made a shared doc where we can put resources and strategies that work. Kai, you can add stuff too if you want.

James: This is actually really smart. I don't want to accidentally make things harder for you because I don't know better.

Priya: Also it just occurred to me that sensory accommodations might help other people too. Like, I have anxiety and the quiet room was really helpful for me as well.

Kai read the messages, feeling something warm expand in his chest. His friends weren't treating his needs as a burden or an inconvenience. They were actively trying to learn and adapt.

He added to the doc:

Some things that help: - Advance notice about plans (surprises are hard for me) - Clear start and end times for activities - Information about the sensory environment (will it be loud? crowded? bright?) - Permission to step away if I need a break - Understanding that sometimes I need recovery time after social stuff

Within an hour, his friends had all read it and added their own notes:

Mia: I didn't know advance notice was important! I'll try to plan stuff further ahead.

James: Added note about asking before hugging or touching—I know I'm a hugger and I should probably check in first.

Priya: I learned that sensory breaks aren't avoiding social time, they're making it possible to actually BE social. Important distinction.

A FEW WEEKS LATER, the friend group was planning a trip to an amusement park. In the old timeline, Kai would have agreed to go and then spent the entire day overwhelmed and miserable. In this new timeline, things went differently.

James: Who's in for Six Flags next month?

Kai: I'm interested but amusement parks are pretty intense sensory environments for me. Can we talk about accommodations?

No anxiety about asking. No shame about having needs.

Mia: Absolutely. What do you need?

Kai: Fast passes so we're not standing in long crowded lines, breaks in quiet areas between rides, permission to skip rides that are too intense, and maybe starting later in the morning when it's less crowded?

Priya: All of that sounds reasonable. I also don't love long lines, so fast passes help me too.

James: And honestly starting later sounds good because I'm not a morning person

Mia: So basically Kai's accommodations make the day better for every-one. Who knew?

Kai smiled at his phone. Who knew, indeed.

The truth was, his friends didn't fully understand what sensory overload felt like. They couldn't—their nervous systems just worked differently. But they didn't need to fully understand in order to respect his needs and make accommodations.

They just needed to care enough to try.

And they did.

~

REFLECT

1. **What sensory experiences are overwhelming or painful for you?**

Be specific. Is it sound (volume, certain frequencies, sudden noises)? Touch (textures, unexpected contact, clothing tags)? Visual (bright lights, fluorescent lighting, patterns)? Smell (strong scents, food smells, chemical smells)? Taste (textures, certain flavors)? Proprioception or vestibular input (movement, balance, body awareness)?

____

____

____

____

____

2. **How do you currently cope with sensory overload?**

Do you avoid situations entirely? Push through and suffer? Have strategies that help? Shut down or melt down afterward? Identify your current coping mechanisms—both helpful and unhelpful.

____

____

____

____

---

3. Have you ever avoided activities you actually wanted to do because of sensory concerns?

Think about times you've said no to friends, missed experiences, or isolated yourself primarily because of sensory overwhelm. How did that feel?

____

____

____

____

____

4. What stops you from asking for sensory accommodations?

Is it fear of judgment? Not knowing what accommodations would help? Believing you should just "deal with it"? Shame about having different needs? Identify the barriers.

____

____

____

____

____

5. What would it feel like to have your sensory needs respected and accommodated?

Imagine friends or family who proactively made accommodations, didn't question your needs, and adjusted plans to include you comfortably. How would that change your social life?

____

____

____

____

∼

ACT

This week, create a personal sensory comfort plan and share it with at least one person you trust.

Step 1: Identify your sensory triggers Create a list organized by sense:

- **Sound triggers:** (examples: loud sudden noises, high-pitched sounds, background noise layers)
- **Visual triggers:** (examples: fluorescent lights, flashing lights, crowds, certain patterns)
- **Touch triggers:** (examples: unexpected touch, certain textures, tight clothing)
- **Smell triggers:** (examples: perfumes, food smells, cleaning products)
- **Taste/texture triggers:** (examples: mixed textures, slimy foods, strong flavors)
- **Other triggers:** (examples: temperature extremes, crowds, unpredictability)

Step 2: Identify your warning signs of sensory overload What does your body do when you're getting overwhelmed?

- Physical signs (tension, shaking, nausea, headache, racing heart)
- Emotional signs (irritability, anxiety, urge to cry or escape)
- Cognitive signs (difficulty processing language, feeling foggy, can't make decisions)
- Behavioral signs (stimming more, going quiet, snapping at people)

Step 3: Identify what helps you regulate

- **Preventative:** What reduces sensory input before overload? (earplugs, sunglasses, fidgets, advance warning, breaks)
- **In the moment:** What helps when you're getting overwhelmed? (quiet space, deep pressure, removing from situation, specific stims)
- **Recovery:** What do you need after sensory overload? (dark quiet room, specific sensory input, sleep, alone time)

Step 4: Create your personal accommodation list Write down specific accommodations that would make challenging environments manageable:

Example: For concerts/loud events: - I need noise-reducing earplugs - I need to be able to step away to a quiet space - I prefer to stay toward the back with more personal space - I need permission to leave early without guilt if it's too much

For social gatherings: - I need advance notice about plans (24-48 hours) - I need to know approximate duration and when I can leave - I need a quiet space where I can take breaks - I do better with smaller groups (4-6 people max)

Step 5: Share this plan with someone Choose one person who cares about you—a friend, family member, partner, or teacher. Share your sensory comfort plan with them. You can:

- Show them the document directly
- Explain it verbally using the document as a guide
- Send it to them digitally with context: "Hey, I wanted to help you understand my sensory needs better. This is what sensory overload feels like for me and what helps."

Step 6: Practice asking for one accommodation this week Pick one situation where you need a sensory accommodation and actually ask for it:

- "Can we meet at the quieter coffee shop instead?"

- "I need to wear my headphones during this—the background noise is overwhelming"
- "Can I step outside for a few minutes? I need a sensory break"
- "Would you mind if we turned down the music/lights?"

Important reminders:

- You don't need to justify or prove your sensory needs are "bad enough" to deserve accommodation
- Accommodations aren't impositions—they're access needs
- People who care about you want you to be comfortable
- Asking for accommodations gets easier with practice
- Not everyone will understand, and that's okay—start with people who are likely to be supportive

Document your experience:

- What accommodation did you ask for?
- How did the person respond?
- Did the accommodation help?
- How did it feel to advocate for your sensory needs?
- What did you learn about yourself or your relationships?

Remember: Your sensory experiences are real and valid. You deserve to participate in activities without suffering. Accommodations aren't special treatment—they're what make inclusion possible.

5

THE ACCOMMODATION CONVERSATION

Priya stared at the English test in front of her, the words swimming and jumping on the page like they always did. She'd studied for hours. She knew this material. But the act of reading the questions, processing them, and formulating written responses while racing against the clock felt like trying to run through water.

Around her, classmates were already on the second page. The girl next to her was writing furiously, her pencil scratching across the paper with confident speed. Priya was still on question three, rereading it for the fourth time because the letters kept rearranging themselves.

She knew she had dyslexia. She'd been diagnosed in third grade. She knew she qualified for accommodations—extended time, the option to use text-to-speech software, a quiet testing environment. Her IEP said she could have these supports.

She'd just never activated them.

The bell rang. Priya had finished maybe half the test. She turned it in, avoiding eye contact with Ms. Chen, and felt the familiar weight of failure settle over her shoulders.

. . .

"Priya, can you stay after class for a moment?" Ms. Chen asked as everyone packed up.

Priya's stomach dropped. She knew what this was about.

When the classroom cleared, Ms. Chen pulled up a chair next to Priya's desk. "I want to talk to you about your test performance."

"I know I did badly—"

"That's not what concerns me," Ms. Chen interrupted gently. "What concerns me is that you're not using the accommodations you're entitled to. According to your IEP, you should have extended time and access to assistive technology for tests and assignments. But you've never once asked for these supports."

Priya looked at her hands. "I don't need them."

"Priya, you scored 43% on this test. But when I look at the questions you did answer, they show deep understanding of the material. Your essays—when you have time to use spell-check and editing tools—are some of the best in the class. You clearly know the content. The problem isn't your knowledge. It's the format."

"I just need to read faster," Priya said quietly.

"You have dyslexia. Your brain processes written language differently. That's not something you can 'just' fix through effort."

"But accommodations feel like cheating."

Ms. Chen sat back. "Why?"

"Because everyone else has to take tests in the regular amount of time without help. If I get extra time and special software, I'm getting an unfair advantage."

"Let me ask you something," Ms. Chen said. "If a student needs glasses to see the board, is that an unfair advantage?"

"No, that's different."

"How is it different?"

Priya struggled to articulate it. "Because... their eyes don't work right. Glasses fix that. But my brain is just slower at reading. That's not the same thing."

"Actually, it is exactly the same thing. Your brain processes written language differently due to dyslexia. Accommodations don't give you an unfair advantage—they level the playing field so you can show what you actually know. Without accommodations, we're not testing your knowledge of English literature. We're testing how fast you can decode text under pressure, which isn't actually the point of the test."

Priya had never thought about it that way.

"I know there's a stigma around accommodations," Ms. Chen continued. "Students worry they'll be seen as less intelligent or less capable. But accommodations aren't about lowering standards. They're about removing barriers that have nothing to do with what we're actually assessing."

"But other students will notice if I'm taking tests in a different room or getting extra time."

"Let them notice. You're not doing anything wrong."

Easy for her to say, Priya thought. She didn't have to be the student who needed special treatment.

THAT NIGHT, Priya's mom brought up the same issue at dinner.

"Your counselor called. She said you're not using your accommodations."

"I don't want to talk about it."

"Priya—"

"I said I don't want to talk about it!" Priya pushed back from the table and went to her room, slamming the door.

She knew she was being unfair. Her mom had fought hard to get her diagnosed, to establish the IEP, to ensure she had legal protections and supports. But her mom didn't understand what it felt like to be different, to be the one who needed special help.

Priya pulled up her favorite online forum for teens with dyslexia. She scrolled through posts from other students:

"My teacher makes a big deal about reading my accommodations out loud in front of the whole class and I want to die"

"A kid told me I was cheating by using speech-to-text. Now I'm too embarrassed to use it"

"I got into my dream college but I'm terrified to ask for accommodations there"

She wasn't alone in her anxiety. But she also saw other posts:

"Finally started using extended time and my grades went from C's to A's. Why did I wait so long?"

"Found a professor who also has dyslexia and she completely normalized it for me"

"Reminder: accommodations aren't special treatment. They're civil rights."

THE NEXT DAY, a new teacher appeared in the English department. Mr. Okafor was young, energetic, and taught the creative writing elective Priya had been considering. During lunch, she saw him in Ms. Chen's classroom, and on impulse, she walked by slowly enough to overhear their conversation.

"—and I always tell students up front that I have dyslexia," Mr. Okafor was saying. "I find that normalizing it early prevents a lot of the accommodation anxiety."

Priya stopped walking. Mr. Okafor had dyslexia?

"Do students ever push back?" Ms. Chen asked.

"Sometimes. Usually it's internalized ableism—they've been told their whole lives that they need to work harder or that accommodations are crutches. I try to reframe it as working smarter, not harder."

Priya knocked on the doorframe. "Sorry to interrupt. Mr. Okafor, I heard you mention dyslexia. I have it too."

Mr. Okafor smiled warmly. "Then you definitely should take my creative writing class next semester. I design all my assignments with dyslexic students in mind—lots of oral storytelling options, speech-to-text friendly prompts, emphasis on revision over perfect first drafts."

"Do you use accommodations?" Priya asked hesitantly.

"Absolutely. I use text-to-speech for most of my reading, speech-to-text for initial drafts, and I give myself extra time for anything that requires intensive reading or writing. I also collaborate with colleagues who are strong copy editors, since my spelling and grammar in first drafts are... creative."

He said it so casually, without shame or apology.

"But you're a teacher," Priya said. "An English teacher. Doesn't it bother you that you need help with reading and writing?"

"Why would it bother me? Dyslexia is just how my brain works. I'm actually a great English teacher because I understand story structure, character development, and theme analysis at a deep level. The dyslexia affects the mechanical processing of text, not my understanding of literature or my ability to teach it. Accommodations let me access and demonstrate my actual skills instead of being limited by decoding challenges."

"Don't people think it's weird that an English teacher has dyslexia?"

"Some people are surprised, sure. But most realize pretty quickly that dyslexia doesn't mean I'm not smart or capable. If anything, it's made me a better teacher because I understand students who struggle with reading and writing. I know what it's like to love stories but find the actual reading process exhausting."

Ms. Chen gave Priya a meaningful look. "Mr. Okafor, could you talk to Priya about accommodations? She's been reluctant to use hers."

MR. OKAFOR INVITED Priya to his classroom during her free period the next day. His walls were covered with student writing samples, visual story maps, and inspirational quotes from famous people with dyslexia—Albert Einstein, Steven Spielberg, Whoopi Goldberg.

"Ms. Chen said you're not using your accommodations," he began. "Can you tell me why?"

Priya explained her fears—about seeming less capable, about other students thinking she was cheating, about drawing attention to her differences.

Mr. Okafor listened carefully. "Okay, I hear you. Those fears are valid and common. But let me tell you what I wish someone had told me when I was your age: refusing to use accommodations doesn't make you seem more capable. It just makes you perform below your actual ability level."

"But I don't want special treatment."

"Accommodations aren't special treatment. Let me give you an analogy. Imagine there's a race, but you're running with a thirty-pound backpack and everyone else is running without one. Accommodations aren't giving you an unfair advantage—they're removing the backpack so you're racing under the same conditions as everyone else."

"But what if people say I'm only doing well because of the accommodations?"

"Then those people don't understand what accommodations are. Look, I publish my writing, I present at conferences, I teach. No one discounts my work because I use assistive technology. The final product is what matters, not the process I use to create it."

He pulled up his computer and showed her his workflow. "See this? This is a paper I'm writing for a journal. I dictated the initial draft using speech-to-text because typing is slow for me. Then I used text-to-speech to read it back to myself so I could hear the flow and catch errors. Then I used grammar-check software to catch spelling and punctuation issues. Then I had a colleague review it. That's my process. And you know what? The final paper is good. The accommodations didn't make it good—they just removed the barriers that would have prevented me from producing it at all."

Priya stared at the screen. She'd always imagined that using accommodations meant producing inferior work, or that the accommodations themselves were doing the work for her. But looking at Mr. Okafor's process, she realized the accommodations were just tools that let him access his own skills.

"What if I start using accommodations now and people notice the change?" she asked.

"Let them notice. 'I'm using the supports I'm legally entitled to' is a complete sentence. You don't owe anyone an explanation beyond that."

"It's scary."

"I know. But you know what's scarier? Spending your entire academic career performing below your ability because you're too afraid to advocate for yourself. Trust me, I did that for years, and I regret it."

THE NEXT DAY, Priya stayed after class and approached Ms. Chen.

"I want to use my accommodations," she said, her voice shaking slightly. "For the next test."

Ms. Chen's face lit up. "I'm so glad to hear that. What accommodations do you want to activate?"

"Extended time. And can I use text-to-speech to read the questions?"

"Absolutely. You'll test in the resource room where you can use headphones and the software without disturbing other students. And you'll have time-and-a-half, which means while the class has 50 minutes, you'll have 75."

"Okay." Priya took a breath. "Okay, let's do it."

TEST DAY ARRIVED. Priya felt self-conscious walking to the resource room instead of staying in the regular classroom, but she forced herself to hold her head up. Mr. Okafor's words echoed in her mind: *You're using the supports you're legally entitled to.*

In the resource room, she put on headphones and started the test. The text-to-speech software read each question aloud while she followed along visually. The combination of hearing and seeing the words made processing so much easier. And with extended time, she didn't feel the usual panic of the clock ticking down while she was still decoding basic sentences.

She moved through the test methodically, actually able to think about her answers instead of just struggling to understand the questions. When she finished, she'd answered every single question—a first for her on timed tests.

A week later, Ms. Chen handed back the graded tests. Priya's paper had a large "91%" written at the top in red ink.

"Much better," Ms. Chen said quietly as she placed the test on Priya's desk. "This is what you're actually capable of when the format isn't the barrier."

Priya stared at the grade. 91%. She'd never scored above an 80% on a timed English test. Ever.

After class, a classmate named Jordan approached her. "Hey, I noticed you tested separately. Do you get extended time?"

Priya's stomach clenched, but she forced herself to meet Jordan's eyes. "Yes. I have dyslexia, so I have accommodations."

"Oh." Jordan paused. "Is that why your grade went up so much?"

Here it was—the accusation she'd been dreading. The implication that her good grade was only because of "special treatment."

But instead of feeling ashamed, Priya felt angry. Angry that she'd spent years performing below her ability because she was afraid of exactly this moment. Angry that people thought accommodations were an unfair advantage instead of basic access.

"My grade went up because I was finally able to show what I actually know," Priya said firmly. "The accommodations don't make the test easier. They remove barriers that have nothing to do with my understanding of the material. I still had to know all the content. I just didn't have to fight my dyslexia at the same time."

Jordan looked uncomfortable. "I didn't mean—"

"I know. But you need to understand that accommodations level the playing field. They don't give me an advantage. They remove a disadvantage."

EMBOLDENED by her success in English, Priya scheduled a meeting with her counselor to review her full IEP and activate accommodations in all her classes. Her counselor was thrilled.

"I've been hoping you'd do this," she said. "You're clearly capable of advanced work, but without accommodations, your grades don't reflect your actual abilities."

They went through each class, identifying which accommodations would be most helpful:

- Extended time on all tests and timed assignments
- Access to text-to-speech software for reading assignments
- Permission to use speech-to-text for essay drafts
- Copies of class notes or slides provided in advance
- Option to demonstrate knowledge through alternate formats when appropriate

"We'll send updated accommodation letters to all your teachers," the counselor explained. "They're required by law to implement these supports."

"What if a teacher doesn't want to?" Priya asked.

"Then you come directly to me, and I'll handle it. Your accommodations are legal rights, not requests."

MOST OF PRIYA'S teachers were supportive. They adjusted their testing procedures, provided materials in accessible formats, and checked in with her about what was working. But her history teacher, Mr. Patterson, was resistant.

"I don't see why you need extended time," he said when Priya approached him before the next test. "All my students take tests in the same amount of time. That's fair."

"Actually, it's not fair," Priya said, surprised by her own confidence. "It's equal, but equal isn't the same as fair. Fair means everyone gets what they need to succeed. I need extended time because of my dyslexia."

"In the real world, you won't get extended time."

"Actually, I will. Standardized tests provide extended time. College entrance exams provide it. Professional licensing exams provide it. The Americans with Disabilities Act requires accommodations in employment. So yes, in the real world, I will get extended time because it's my legal right."

Mr. Patterson looked taken aback. "I just don't want you to become dependent on accommodations."

"Would you tell a student with glasses that they shouldn't become 'dependent' on them?" Priya countered. "Accommodations aren't crutches. They're tools that let me access my education. I'm not asking you to lower your standards or make the test easier. I'm asking you to implement the legally mandated supports that are already in my IEP."

"I'll need to verify this with the counselor."

"Please do. She'll confirm everything I've told you."

AFTER HER MEETING with the counselor confirmed Priya's rights, Mr. Patterson reluctantly provided the accommodations. Priya took the history test in the resource room with extended time, and once again, her performance improved dramatically.

Word got around that Priya was advocating for herself. A freshman with ADHD approached her in the hallway.

"I heard you stood up to Mr. Patterson about accommodations," the girl said shyly. "I have accommodations too, but I've been too scared to use them. How did you get brave enough?"

Priya thought about it. "I realized that not using accommodations doesn't make me braver or more capable. It just makes me struggle unnecessarily. And I met a teacher with dyslexia who helped me understand that accommodations are tools, not cheats."

"I'm scared people will think I'm dumb."

"Some people might think that. Those people are wrong. Anyone who understands what accommodations actually are knows they don't reflect your intelligence—they reflect your access needs."

The girl nodded slowly. "Maybe I'll try using mine."

"You should. You deserve to show what you're actually capable of."

. . .

By the end of the semester, Priya's grades had improved across the board. Her GPA jumped from a 3.0 to a 3.7. Her standardized test scores—taken with accommodations—put her in range for competitive colleges. Teachers who had previously seen her as an average student suddenly recognized her potential.

But the biggest change wasn't in her grades. It was in how she saw herself.

She wasn't broken or deficient. She wasn't less intelligent than her peers. She just learned differently, and she needed different tools to access her education. Once she accepted that and advocated for what she needed, everything changed.

At her IEP meeting that spring, Priya spoke up about her transition planning for college.

"I want to make sure I understand how to set up accommodations in college," she said. "Because I'm going to need them there too."

Her mom looked like she might cry. For years, she'd watched Priya struggle and refuse help. Seeing her daughter finally advocate for herself was clearly emotional.

"That's very mature," the counselor said. "College accommodations work differently than high school—you have to self-advocate and connect with disability services yourself. But with your experience advocating here, I think you'll handle it well."

After the meeting, Mr. Okafor pulled Priya aside.

"I heard you stood up to Mr. Patterson. I'm proud of you."

"You helped me understand that I wasn't asking for special treatment."

"You weren't. And you know what? Every time you advocate for yourself, you're making it a little bit easier for the next student with dyslexia to do the same. You're normalizing accommodation use. That matters."

Priya hadn't thought about it that way—that her self-advocacy could help other students too.

"I wish I'd started using accommodations sooner," she admitted.

"That's a common regret. But you're using them now, and you're teaching other students that it's okay to ask for what they need. That's what matters."

On the last day of school, Priya signed up for Mr. Okafor's creative writing class for the following year. She also volunteered to be a peer mentor for incoming students with learning differences, helping them understand their IEPs and feel less alone.

She'd spent years seeing her dyslexia as a shameful secret, something to hide and overcome. Now she understood it was just a different way of processing information—one that required accommodations to access education on equal footing with her peers.

The accommodations didn't make her less capable. They revealed her actual capabilities.

And she was done apologizing for needing them.

~

REFLECT

1. What accommodations do you need but aren't using? Why not?

Be honest about what supports would help you—at school, at work, in daily life—and what stops you from accessing them. Is it shame? Fear of judgment? Not knowing what's available? Belief that you should "handle it" on your own?

____

____

____

____

____

2. Do you view accommodations as "special treatment" or as access needs?

Examine your own beliefs about accommodations. Do you see

them as giving you an unfair advantage, or as leveling the playing field? Where do these beliefs come from?

____

____

____

____

____

3. Have you ever performed below your ability because you weren't using needed accommodations?

Think about times when you struggled unnecessarily—not because you didn't know the material or couldn't do the task, but because the format or environment created barriers you could have removed with accommodations.

____

____

____

____

____

4. What would it take for you to feel comfortable advocating for your accommodation needs?

Is it information about your rights? Role models who use accommodations? Practice with the language of self-advocacy? Support from specific people? Identify what you need to feel empowered to ask.

____

____

____

____

____

. . .

5. How might your accommodation use (or non-use) affect other people with similar needs?

Consider Priya's realization that her self-advocacy normalized accommodations for other students. When you hide your needs or refuse accommodations, what message does that send to others who are watching?

____

____

____

____

____

~

ACT

This week, identify one accommodation you need and practice asking for it.

Step 1: Identify what you need

Choose ONE accommodation that would genuinely help you. Don't try to tackle everything at once. Examples:

- Extended time on tests or assignments
- Text-to-speech or speech-to-text software
- Preferential seating (front of class, away from distractions, near door for breaks)
- Note-taking support
- Breaks during long tasks
- Quiet testing environment
- Assignment instructions in writing
- Advance access to materials
- Alternate format for demonstrating knowledge

Step 2: Know your rights

Research what you're legally entitled to:

- If you're in school (K-12): You may qualify for a 504 plan or IEP
- If you're in college: You have rights under ADA and Section 504—connect with disability services
- If you're employed: You have rights under ADA to reasonable accommodations
- For standardized tests: Most offer accommodations with documentation

Knowing your rights makes advocacy feel less like begging and more like accessing what's already yours.

Step 3: Prepare your language

Practice what you'll say. Use clear, factual language:

"I have [condition] and I need [specific accommodation] to access [task/material] on equal footing. This is covered under [my IEP/504 plan/ADA/etc.]."

Examples:

- "I have dyslexia and I need extended time on tests. This accommodation is in my IEP."
- "I have ADHD and I need a quiet environment for focused work. Can we discuss what that might look like?"
- "I'm autistic and I need advance notice about schedule changes to manage transitions effectively."

Step 4: Identify who to ask

Who has the authority to grant your accommodation?

- Teacher/professor
- Disability services coordinator
- School counselor
- HR representative
- Supervisor/manager

Go to the right person. If someone says no, escalate to the next level—your accommodations are rights, not requests.

Step 5: Make the ask

Actually do it. Request a brief meeting, send an email, or speak up in the moment. You can:

- Request it verbally in person
- Send an email (which creates a paper trail)
- Have a parent/advocate with you if needed
- Connect with disability services who can facilitate

Step 6: If you face pushback, stand firm

Not everyone will understand or comply immediately. Prepare for potential pushback:

If someone says it's "unfair to other students": "Accommodations level the playing field. They don't give me an advantage—they remove a barrier that has nothing to do with what you're actually assessing."

If someone says "you'll become dependent": "Would you tell someone with glasses they'll become dependent on them? Accommodations are tools that let me access my abilities, not crutches that weaken me."

If someone says "in the real world you won't get accommodations": "Actually, accommodations are legally protected in employment, higher education, and professional licensing. And more importantly, we're not preparing for a world that excludes disabled people—we're creating a world that includes us."

If someone refuses to implement legally mandated accommodations: "I need you to understand that these aren't requests—they're legal requirements under [specific law]. If you're unable to implement them, I'll need to escalate this to [disability services coordinator/school administrator/HR]."

Step 7: Document everything

Keep records of:

- Accommodation requests (emails, meeting notes)

- Who you spoke with and when
- What accommodations were agreed to
- Any denial or pushback

Documentation protects your rights if you need to advocate further.

Step 8: Reflect on the experience

After you ask for your accommodation:

- How did it feel to advocate for yourself?
- How did the person respond?
- Did you get the accommodation you requested?
- What would you do differently next time?
- How will this accommodation change your performance or wellbeing?

Extension challenge:

Once you're comfortable using one accommodation, add another. Build your self-advocacy skills progressively. Eventually, accommodation use will feel normal and automatic rather than scary and shameful.

Also consider: Can you help normalize accommodations for others? Maybe by:

- Being open about your accommodation use (reduces stigma)
- Encouraging other students to use their supports
- Educating peers about what accommodations actually are
- Challenging ableist comments when you hear them

Remember:

- Accommodations are not special treatment—they're access

- You're not asking for an unfair advantage—you're asking to remove an unfair disadvantage
- Needing accommodations doesn't mean you're less capable—it means you're self-aware and resourceful
- Self-advocacy is a skill that improves with practice
- You deserve to perform at your actual ability level, not at the level your disability allows without support

You have a right to access. Use it.

6

SPECIAL INTEREST, SPECIAL LIFE

Devon's bedroom looked like a marine biology research lab had exploded. Posters of ocean ecosystems covered every wall—coral reefs, deep sea trenches, kelp forests, hydrothermal vents. His bookshelves overflowed with field guides, scientific journals, and marine biology textbooks he'd collected from used bookstores and library sales. A 40-gallon saltwater aquarium bubbled in the corner, home to carefully maintained coral fragments and a cleaner shrimp Devon had named Dr. Shrimpton.

His desk was covered in detailed drawings of marine species, notes on ocean acidification, and printouts of recent research papers on coral bleaching. Devon had organized his entire digital life around marine biology too—his phone wallpaper was a whale shark, his playlists were named after ocean zones, and his social media followed exclusively marine biologists, oceanographers, and conservation organizations.

At fifteen, Devon had already decided his entire life trajectory: marine biology degree, PhD in coral reef ecology, career in marine conservation. He knew exactly which universities had the best programs, which professors were doing the most interesting research, and what the current debates in the field were.

His parents called it an obsession. His teachers called it "lacking balance." His school counselor suggested he "diversify his interests." Even his friends sometimes got a glazed look when Devon started talking about the symbiotic relationships in coral reef ecosystems.

But to Devon, marine biology wasn't just an interest. It was his world, his passion, the thing that made life make sense.

"DEVON, we need to talk about your course selection for next year," his mom said at dinner one evening.

Devon looked up from the marine biology documentary playing on his tablet. "What about it?"

"You've signed up for AP Biology, AP Environmental Science, and Marine Science. That's three science classes."

"And?"

"And you need a more well-rounded education. What about art? Or a second language? Or business classes?"

"I don't want to take those. I want to study marine biology."

His dad joined in. "We understand you're interested in marine life, but you're putting all your eggs in one basket. What if you change your mind about marine biology?"

"I won't."

"You're fifteen. You might. And then you'll have no other developed interests or skills."

Devon felt frustration rising. "Why is it bad to know what I want? Everyone's always telling teenagers to 'find their passion' and 'pursue their dreams,' but when I actually have a passion and pursue it, suddenly it's 'too much' and I need 'balance.'"

"It's not about it being bad," his mom said carefully. "It's about being realistic. Most people don't end up working in their teenage interests. We just want you to have options."

"I don't want options. I want marine biology."

His parents exchanged that look—the one that said they thought Devon was being stubborn and would eventually see reason.

"Just think about it," his dad said. "Maybe take one non-science elective. Show some variety."

THE NEXT DAY AT SCHOOL, Devon's English teacher pulled him aside.

"Devon, I noticed you wrote your personal essay about coral reef conservation again."

"The prompt was about something we're passionate about."

"Yes, but this is the third essay you've written about marine biology this semester. Don't you have any other interests?"

"Not really, no."

Ms. Rodriguez sighed. "Devon, colleges want to see well-rounded students. Students with diverse interests and activities. If all your essays, projects, and extracurriculars are about marine biology, you're going to look... narrow."

"But isn't depth better than breadth? Isn't it good that I'm really committed to something?"

"In moderation, yes. But there's a thing called being too specialized too early. You're only fifteen. You should be exploring different subjects, trying new things."

Devon left the conversation feeling frustrated and misunderstood. Why was everyone so determined to pull him away from the thing he loved? Why was deep interest seen as a problem rather than a strength?

At lunch, he sat with his friends and tried to join the conversation about the latest Netflix show everyone was watching.

"Did you see episode four?" Mia asked excitedly.

"I haven't started it yet," Devon admitted.

"Wait, seriously? Everyone's watching it!"

"I've been watching this documentary series about deep sea exploration. It's incredible—they found new species of octopus near hydrothermal vents, and the footage of—"

"Devon," James interrupted gently. "Maybe not everyone wants to hear about octopuses right now."

Devon felt his face heat up. He did this all the time—hijacked conversations to talk about marine life even when no one asked. His friends were nice about it, but Devon could tell it bothered them.

"Sorry," Devon mumbled.

"It's okay," Mia said. "We just wish you were interested in some of the same stuff we're interested in, you know? So we could actually talk about it together."

Devon nodded but felt something twist in his chest. He wished he could care about the things his friends cared about. But his brain just... didn't work that way. Netflix shows and celebrity drama felt like empty noise compared to the fascinating complexity of marine ecosystems.

THAT WEEKEND, Devon's parents forced him to attend a career fair at the community center.

"Just explore some different options," his mom said. "You might discover something new you're interested in."

Devon trudged through booths for engineering, medicine, law, business, education. Everyone was enthusiastic about their careers, but nothing sparked even a flicker of interest. Until he reached a booth tucked in the corner: Marine Conservation Initiative.

Behind the table sat a woman in her early thirties wearing a t-shirt with a sea turtle on it. Her booth was covered with stunning underwater photography.

"Hi there," she said as Devon approached. "I'm Dr. Chen. Marine biologist and conservation photographer. You look like you might actually be interested, unlike the last twenty people who walked by."

"I am," Devon said, feeling suddenly energized. "I want to be a marine biologist. I've wanted to be one since I was eight."

Dr. Chen's eyes lit up. "Since you were eight? That's commitment. What's your specific interest?"

"Coral reef ecology. Specifically the impacts of climate change and ocean acidification on reef systems, and potential intervention strategies."

Dr. Chen blinked. "Wow. Okay. That's... very specific for a high schooler. How much do you know about current research?"

Devon launched into an enthusiastic explanation of recent studies he'd read, ongoing debates about coral restoration approaches, and his own theories about scalable conservation strategies. He pulled up photos on his phone of his home aquarium and explained his coral propagation experiments.

Ten minutes later, Devon finally paused to breathe.

"Sorry," he said automatically. "I info dump sometimes. I know it's annoying."

"Annoying?" Dr. Chen looked genuinely confused. "That was one of the most informed and passionate explanations of coral ecology I've heard from anyone, including my graduate students. Why would that be annoying?"

"Because... people don't usually want to hear about marine biology for ten minutes straight?"

"People who aren't interested in marine biology don't want to hear about it," Dr. Chen corrected. "But people who are interested in marine biology—people like me—love exactly that kind of enthusiastic deep dive. Pun intended."

Devon laughed despite himself.

"Can I tell you something?" Dr. Chen said. "I'm autistic. And when I was your age, everyone told me I was 'too obsessed' with marine life. My parents wanted me to have 'balance.' My teachers wanted me to 'broaden my interests.' My friends thought I was boring because I only wanted to talk about ocean stuff."

"What did you do?"

"I ignored them. I went all-in on marine biology. I did three science internships in high school, all marine-focused. I went to college specifically for their marine program. I did my PhD on coral reef resilience. Now I run a conservation organization and get paid to do exactly what I love."

"But everyone says I should be well-rounded."

"Well-rounded is overrated," Dr. Chen said firmly. "You know what colleges and employers actually want? Expertise. Passion. Deep knowledge. Someone who's genuinely committed to a field and has been building expertise in it for years. That's way more valuable than someone who dabbled in everything but never went deep in anything."

"Really?"

"Really. Look, here's the thing about special interests—and I'm using that term deliberately because I assume you know it—they're actually a superpower for autistic people. That ability to hyperfocus, to retain massive amounts of information, to notice patterns and details others miss, to sustain interest over years? That's what creates experts. That's what drives innovation. That's what leads to break-through research."

Devon felt something release in his chest—a tension he'd been carrying for so long he'd stopped noticing it.

"Everyone acts like my focus on marine biology is a problem," he said quietly.

"It's only a problem if you let other people convince you it is," Dr. Chen said. "I'm not saying you shouldn't take required classes or develop basic life skills. But this idea that you need to artificially develop interest in things you don't care about just to seem 'well-rounded'? That's nonsense. Lean into your strengths. Develop your expertise. The world needs people who care deeply about things, not people who care a little bit about everything."

Dr. Chen gave Devon her email address and invited him to volunteer at a local beach cleanup the organization was running the following month. Devon left the career fair feeling more validated than he had in months.

That night, he brought up the conversation at dinner.

"I met a marine biologist today. She said my focus on marine biology is actually a strength, not a problem."

His parents exchanged glances. "Devon—"

"She's autistic too," Devon continued. "She said her special interest in marine life is what made her successful in her career. That deep focus and expertise is what colleges and employers actually want."

"That's one person's opinion," his mom said carefully.

"Maybe. But it made me think about something. You're always saying I need balance and diverse interests. But neither of you have that. Dad, you've been an accountant for twenty years. You're specialized. Mom, you've worked in nursing your whole career. You're specialized. Why is it okay for you to have focused careers but not okay for me to have a focused interest?"

His parents were quiet.

"I'm not saying I won't take required classes," Devon said. "I'll take English and math and history. But I don't want to waste elective slots on things I don't care about just to seem well-rounded. I want to use every possible opportunity to build my expertise in marine biology. Because that's what I'm good at. That's what I love. That's what I want to do with my life."

His dad sighed. "You make a fair point. I think we're just worried about you limiting your options."

"I'm not limiting my options. I'm choosing my option. That's different."

OVER THE NEXT FEW MONTHS, Devon doubled down on his marine biology focus instead of diluting it. He:

- Kept all three science classes in his schedule
- Started volunteering with Dr. Chen's conservation organization
- Began a research project on local tide pool ecosystems
- Started a marine conservation club at school
- Applied for a summer internship at the local aquarium

Instead of trying to hide his enthusiasm or apologize for his info dumps, he started seeking out spaces and people who appreciated his deep knowledge.

At the conservation organization's beach cleanup, Devon met other volunteers who were genuinely interested in marine life. When he explained the ecological importance of removing plastic from beaches, people listened intently and asked follow-up questions.

"You really know your stuff," one volunteer said admiringly.

"Thanks. Marine biology is kind of my thing."

"Have you considered leading educational tours at the beach? We're always looking for knowledgeable volunteers to teach visitors about tide pool ecology."

Devon's eyes widened. People wanted to hear him talk about marine life? For extended periods? On purpose?

He started leading monthly tide pool tours, where his tendency to info dump became an actual asset. Visitors were fascinated by Devon's ability to identify every species, explain complex ecological relationships, and share current conservation challenges.

"That was amazing," a parent told Devon after one tour. "My son usually gets bored on these educational things, but you made it so interesting. Have you thought about becoming a teacher or naturalist?"

The idea had never occurred to Devon. He'd always focused on research and conservation. But education—sharing his passion with people who wanted to learn—felt incredibly fulfilling.

At school, Devon's marine conservation club attracted other students with niche interests. Some were into birds, some into native plants, some into climate science. They weren't all autistic, but many were neurodivergent, and all of them appreciated having a space where deep interest in specific topics was celebrated rather than judged.

"I love that you just talk about marine stuff without apologizing," one club member said. "Everyone else in my life tells me I talk about plants too much."

"People told me that about marine biology," Devon said. "But then

I found people who actually want to hear about it. Those are my people."

Devon still had friends who weren't into marine biology. He still hung out with Mia and James and the usual group. But Devon stopped apologizing for his enthusiasm. If the conversation turned to shows he hadn't watched, he'd participate where he could and excuse himself when he couldn't contribute. If an opportunity arose to share something marine-related, he'd gauge interest and share appropriately—but without the constant self-censoring he used to do.

"You seem happier lately," Mia observed one day.

"I am," Devon said. "I stopped trying to be interested in things I'm not interested in. It's kind of freeing."

"That makes sense. I'm sorry if we made you feel bad about the marine biology stuff. It's actually cool that you're so passionate about something."

"Thanks. And I'm sorry I used to hijack every conversation. I'm getting better at reading whether people actually want to hear about octopuses or if they're just being polite."

Mia laughed. "For the record, I do sometimes want to hear about octopuses. Just maybe not every single day."

"Fair enough."

THE SUMMER BEFORE JUNIOR YEAR, Devon started his internship at the local aquarium. On his first day, the education director introduced him to the other teen interns.

"This is Devon. He's going to be working primarily with our coral reef exhibit and tide pool touch tank. Devon has extensive knowledge of marine ecology—probably more than some of our staff—so don't hesitate to ask him questions."

Devon felt his chest swell with pride. His knowledge was an asset here, not a problem.

He was assigned to shadow a senior educator named Marcus, who turned out to be autistic and had a special interest in cephalopods.

"Oh thank god, another person who actually cares about the science," Marcus said when they met. "Last summer's intern spent the whole time on their phone and couldn't tell visitors the difference between a sea star and a sea urchin."

Over the summer, Devon learned to channel his info-dumping into structured educational presentations. He discovered he was really good at reading audiences—knowing when to go deep into scientific detail and when to keep things simple and engaging.

"You're a natural educator," Marcus told him. "Have you thought about marine biology education as a career path? We need more educators who actually understand and care about the science."

Devon hadn't considered it seriously before, but the idea took root. Maybe he didn't have to choose between research and sharing his passion. Maybe he could do both—research that informed conservation, education that inspired others to care about marine ecosystems.

When school started junior year, Devon's college counselor called him in to discuss his application strategy.

"I'm concerned about your course load," the counselor said, looking at Devon's schedule. "You're very science-heavy. Colleges like to see balance."

"Actually," Devon said confidently, "I've been researching what marine biology programs look for in applicants. They want demonstrated long-term commitment to the field, evidence of independent research, real-world experience, and deep knowledge. My specialized focus is exactly what they're looking for."

The counselor looked skeptical. "That's a very specific strategy."

"It's a strategy backed by conversations with marine biologists, aquarium educators, and research from admission departments of the programs I'm interested in." Devon pulled out printed materials. "Look—here's UC Santa Barbara's marine biology program admission page. They explicitly say they're looking for students with sustained interest and experience in marine science. Same with

Scripps Institution of Oceanography. Same with University of Hawaii."

The counselor reviewed the materials. "I stand corrected. You've clearly done your research."

"Marine biology is kind of my thing," Devon said with a slight smile.

By the end of junior year, Devon's college application was taking shape:

Academics: Rigorous science focus, particularly in marine/environmental sciences **Experience:** Three years volunteering with marine conservation organization, two summers aquarium internship, independent research project **Leadership:** Founded and led school marine conservation club **Essays:** All focused on his passion for coral reef ecology and conservation **Recommendations:** From Dr. Chen and the aquarium director, both emphasizing Devon's expertise and dedication

It wasn't well-rounded in the traditional sense. It was deeply focused. And according to every marine biology program he researched, that was exactly what they wanted to see.

When Dr. Chen reviewed Devon's application materials, she smiled.

"This is going to make you stand out. You're not another student who dabbled in science and did generically impressive things. You're someone who's been building genuine expertise in a specific field since you were a kid. That's memorable. That's valuable."

"I used to think my focus on marine biology was a bad thing."

"It's only a bad thing if you let people who don't understand neurodivergent minds define what's valuable," Dr. Chen said. "Your special interest isn't a quirk or a phase. It's the foundation of your future expertise. Lean into it. Own it. Let it be the thing that makes you remarkable."

.   .   .

DEVON'S PARENTS came around eventually. Watching their son thrive once they stopped trying to force "balance" was convincing in a way that arguments never could be.

"I think we owe you an apology," Devon's mom said one evening. "We were so focused on what we thought you should be interested in that we didn't appreciate what you actually are interested in. And clearly it's working for you."

"It is," Devon agreed. "But I understand why you were worried. Society tells parents that specialized kids are at risk. That we need to be well-rounded. But that model doesn't work for everyone, especially not for autistic people whose special interests are literally part of how our brains work."

"We're proud of you," his dad said. "Not just for your accomplishments, but for knowing yourself well enough to stick with what matters to you even when everyone was pushing you in different directions."

SENIOR YEAR, Devon applied to six marine biology programs. His essays all focused unapologetically on his deep commitment to coral reef conservation. His recommendations all emphasized his unusual depth of knowledge for a high school student. His interview with Scripps went exceptionally well—he spent forty-five minutes discussing coral bleaching mechanisms with a professor who appreciated his grasp of current research.

When acceptance letters started arriving in the spring, Devon got into five of his six choices, including his top pick: Scripps Institution of Oceanography.

The acceptance letter specifically mentioned his "demonstrated sustained commitment to marine science" and "impressive depth of knowledge for an undergraduate applicant."

Devon read the letter three times, then called Dr. Chen.

"I got in. I got into Scripps."

"Of course you did. You're exactly the kind of student they're looking for—someone who's been building expertise and genuine passion for years. Congratulations, Devon. You earned this."

That night, Devon sat in front of his aquarium, watching Dr. Shrimpton clean the coral fragments he'd been nurturing for two years. He thought about all the times he'd been told he was too focused, too specialized, too obsessed.

He thought about how he'd almost believed it. Almost let other people convince him that his deep interest was a problem rather than a strength.

But he hadn't. He'd found people like Dr. Chen who understood that special interests weren't limitations—they were launching pads for expertise, innovation, and fulfillment.

Devon was going to study coral reef ecology at one of the world's premier marine science institutions. He was going to build a career around the thing he'd loved since he was eight years old.

His special interest hadn't been too much. It had been exactly enough.

~

REFLECT

1. What is your special interest or deep passion?

Be honest about what captivates you, even if others have told you it's "too much" or you should "have balance." What topic, hobby, or field could you talk about for hours? What do you naturally gravitate toward when you have free time and energy?

____

____

____

____

____

2. How have people responded to your special interest?

Have you been told you're too obsessed, too focused, too one-track? That you need to "broaden your horizons" or "diversify your interests"? Have people dismissed your passion as a phase or suggested you should care about what they care about instead?

____

____

____

____

____

3. Do you hide or minimize your enthusiasm about your special interest? Why?

Think about whether you apologize for info dumping, avoid bringing up your interest, or pretend to care about things you don't actually care about to fit in. What fears drive this behavior?

____

____

____

____

____

4. Have you ever met someone who shares your special interest or appreciates your deep knowledge?

Recall moments when someone actually wanted to hear you talk about your passion, when your expertise was valued, or when you connected with others over shared interests. How did those experiences feel different?

____

____

____

____

____

. . .

5. How might your life look different if you leaned into your special interest instead of trying to suppress or balance it?

Imagine building your education, career, and community around your passion. What becomes possible when you stop apologizing for your deep focus?

____

____

____

____

____

∼

ACT

This week, deliberately lean into your special interest without apology.

Step 1: Identify your special interest

If it's not immediately obvious, ask yourself:

- What do I think about when my mind wanders?
- What topics could I discuss for hours without getting bored?
- What do I research or learn about in my free time?
- What makes me lose track of time when I'm engaged with it?
- What do people tell me I talk about "too much"?

Step 2: Stop apologizing for it

Notice how often you:

- Apologize before sharing something about your interest ("Sorry, I know I talk about this too much, but...")
- Minimize your enthusiasm ("I'm kind of into ______")
- Self-censor by not bringing it up even when relevant
- Feel shame about the depth of your knowledge or passion

This week, practice sharing without apologizing. When something related to your interest comes up, contribute your knowledge naturally. Let yourself be enthusiastic.

Step 3: Spend intentional, guilt-free time on your special interest

Dedicate at least 2-3 hours this week to your special interest without:

- Feeling like you "should" be doing something more productive
- Forcing yourself to do "balanced" activities first to "earn" it
- Apologizing to others for spending time on it
- Justifying it as "research" or "for school" when it's really just for you

Step 4: Find (or create) a space where your special interest is welcomed

Look for:

- Online communities focused on your interest (Reddit, Discord, specialized forums)
- Local clubs, classes, or meetup groups
- Volunteer opportunities related to your interest
- Social media accounts/hashtags where people share your passion
- One person in your life who genuinely wants to hear about it

If you can't find a space, consider creating one:

- Start a club at school
- Create an online group or account dedicated to the topic
- Propose a research project or independent study focused on your interest

Step 5: Info dump proudly (in appropriate contexts)
Practice reading your audience:

- In dedicated spaces (clubs, forums, people who share your interest): Info dump freely
- With friends/family who show genuine interest: Share enthusiastically when they ask
- In general social situations: Gauge interest and share in proportion to engagement

The key: Stop seeing info dumping as inherently bad. It's only inappropriate when the audience isn't interested. Find audiences who ARE interested, and then talk as much as you want.

Step 6: Explore how your special interest could connect to your future
Research:

- What careers exist in this field?
- What education or training is required?
- Who are the experts? (Follow them, read their work, reach out if appropriate)
- What problems in this field need solving?
- How can deep focus on this topic create value?

You don't have to commit to a career path, but explore the possibility that your special interest could be more than a hobby—it could be your life's work.

Step 7: Document your experience
At the end of the week, reflect:

- How did it feel to engage with your special interest without guilt?
- Did you find any welcoming spaces or communities?
- How did people respond when you shared enthusiastically?

- What possibilities opened up when you stopped apologizing?
- How might your relationship with your special interest change going forward?

Important reminders:

- Your special interest is not "too much"—it's exactly right for your brain
- Deep focus is a superpower, not a problem
- Expertise comes from sustained interest, not scattered dabbling
- The world needs people who care deeply about specific things
- Your enthusiasm is valuable to people who share your interest
- You don't need to be "well-rounded" to be successful—you need to be deeply knowledgeable

Extension challenge:

Reach out to one expert or professional in your field of interest. Send an email expressing your passion and asking one thoughtful question. Many experts love hearing from enthusiastic young people and are willing to share advice, resources, or encouragement.

Example: *"Dear Dr. [Name], I'm a high school student with a deep interest in [field]. I've been following your work on [specific topic] and was fascinated by [specific thing]. I'm hoping to pursue [field] professionally and wondered if you had any advice for building expertise at my age. Thank you for your work in this field."*

You might be surprised by who responds—and how much they appreciate your genuine enthusiasm.

7

———————

SOCIAL SCRIPTS & DATING

Aria knew she'd said something wrong the moment Olivia's face changed. Her smile disappeared, replaced by a tight expression Aria had learned meant "offended" or "hurt."

"What?" Aria asked, genuinely confused.

"Nothing," Olivia said in a tone that clearly meant "something."

"No, seriously, what did I say?"

"If you don't know, I'm not going to explain it to you." Olivia gathered her lunch and moved to a different table.

Aria sat there, bewildered, mentally replaying the conversation. They'd been talking about Olivia's presentation in history class. Olivia had asked how it went, and Aria had been honest: "I thought your introduction was really strong, but the middle section dragged a bit and you probably could have cut three slides to make it tighter."

That was... honest feedback, right? Olivia had asked. Aria had answered. What was wrong with that?

This kept happening. Aria would say something she thought was straightforward and helpful, and people would get upset. She'd ask a clarifying question and people would call her rude. She'd skip social niceties to get to the point and people would say she was "too blunt" or "socially awkward."

Being autistic meant Aria's brain processed social interaction differently than neurotypical people. The unwritten rules that everyone else seemed to intuitively understand were completely invisible to Aria. It was like everyone had been given a manual for social interaction except her, and she was expected to figure it out through trial and error—with each error costing her friendships.

THAT EVENING, Aria vented to her older sister, Maya, who was home from college for the weekend.

"I don't understand what I did wrong," Aria said. "Olivia asked for my opinion. I gave it. She got mad."

"What exactly did you say?" Maya asked.

Aria repeated her comment about the presentation.

Maya winced. "Okay, I see the problem."

"What? I was being helpful!"

"When someone asks 'how did I do?' right after a presentation, they're not actually asking for critical feedback. They're asking for reassurance and support."

"But she literally asked how it went."

"Right, but neurotypical communication has this whole subtext layer. When people ask certain questions in certain contexts, they're not looking for literal answers. They're looking for emotional support."

Aria felt frustration building. "That makes no sense. If you want emotional support, say 'I need reassurance about my presentation.' Don't ask 'how did I do?' if you don't actually want to know."

"I agree it's confusing," Maya said sympathetically. "But that's how neurotypical social scripts work. There's what people say, and then there's what they mean, and you're supposed to figure out the difference from context."

"But I can't read context! That's literally part of being autistic!"

"I know. Which is why you need a translation guide."

· · ·

MAYA EXPLAINED that when she'd first started college, she'd struggled with similar social confusion. Her roommate, who was also autistic, had created what they called a "neurotypical translation guide"—a document where they recorded confusing social situations and broke down the unwritten rules.

"It's like learning a foreign language," Maya said. "You have to study the patterns until they become recognizable."

She pulled up her old guide on her laptop and showed Aria:

COMPLIMENTS/FEEDBACK RULES:

- If someone shows you something they made (art, writing, presentation), start with positive comments even if you see problems
- "That's interesting!" is a safe response when you don't know what else to say
- If they specifically ask "what could be better?" then you can offer constructive criticism
- If they just ask "what do you think?" stick to positive observations

QUESTIONS THAT AREN'T REALLY QUESTIONS:

- "How are you?" = greeting, not actual question about wellbeing. Answer: "Good, how are you?"
- "Can I ask you a question?" = they're going to ask anyway, just say "sure"
- "Do you want to hang out sometime?" = they're asking if you're interested, not for an immediate time commitment

THINGS PEOPLE SAY VS. WHAT THEY MEAN:

- "No offense, but..." = they're about to say something offensive
- "We should hang out!" = polite ending to conversation, not actual plan

- "It's fine" in an annoyed tone = it's not fine
- "Whatever you want" = they have a preference but want you to guess it

Aria stared at the guide. "This is so much work just to have basic conversations."

"Yeah," Maya agreed. "It is. And it's not fair that autistic people have to do all this extra labor to navigate neurotypical social rules while neurotypical people don't have to learn our communication style at all."

"So what do I do?"

"You have a few options. One: learn enough neurotypical social scripts to avoid the worst misunderstandings. Two: find friends who communicate more directly and don't require all this translation. Three: be upfront about being autistic and needing direct communication. Ideally, some combination of all three."

ARIA STARTED her own social translation guide. Every time she had a confusing interaction, she'd write it down and try to decode the unwritten rule she'd missed. She also started asking her friend Riley, who was particularly patient and direct, to help her understand social situations.

"Hey Riley, can I ask you something?" Aria said at lunch a few days later.

"Sure."

"Yesterday in English, when Mr. Johnson asked if anyone had questions about the assignment, I asked three follow-up questions. After class, someone told me I was 'monopolizing class time.' Was I supposed to know to stop asking questions after a certain number?"

Riley thought about it. "Kind of, yeah. The unwritten rule is that you can ask one or two questions, but if you have more than that, you're supposed to ask the teacher privately after class or during office hours."

"Why?"

"Because other people might have questions too, or want class to end on time, and if one person asks too many questions, it affects everyone else."

"But wouldn't it be more efficient if everyone just asked all their questions at once so the teacher only has to explain once?"

"Logically, yes. Socially, no. People get annoyed when they perceive someone as taking up too much time or attention."

Aria added this to her guide under a new section: **CLASSROOM SOCIAL RULES - Don't ask more than 2 questions in class, save detailed questions for after class or office hours.**

It was exhausting, documenting all these invisible rules. But at least when Aria reviewed her guide before social situations, she could avoid some of the worst mistakes.

EVERYTHING GOT MORE complicated when Aria developed a crush on Jordan, a classmate in her physics class.

Jordan was smart, funny, and didn't seem bothered by Aria's direct communication style. They'd been lab partners for a month, and Aria had started looking forward to physics more than any other class.

One day, Jordan said, "We should study together for the exam. Want to come over this weekend?"

Aria's heart jumped. "Yes, that would be efficient since we can quiz each other."

"Cool. Saturday at 2?"

"That works with my schedule."

After Jordan left, Aria's friend Casey pulled her aside.

"Jordan totally likes you," Casey said.

"We're study partners. Of course we like working together."

"No, I mean *likes* you. That was her asking you out."

"She asked me to study. For physics."

Casey laughed. "Studying together is date code for spending time alone together. This is a romantic thing."

Aria felt panic rising. "How was I supposed to know that? She said 'study for the exam.' That sounds like academic collaboration, not a date."

"Context, Aria. You two have been flirting for weeks."

"Have we?" Aria had no idea if she'd been flirting. She'd been discussing physics concepts and enjoying Jordan's company. Was that flirting?

Aria went to Maya in crisis mode.

"I think someone asked me on a date but I'm not sure and I don't know how dating works and I'm going to mess this up," Aria said in one breath.

Maya laughed gently. "Okay, slow down. Tell me what happened."

Aria explained the study session situation.

"That does sound like it could be a date," Maya confirmed. "Or it could genuinely be studying. The way to know is to clarify directly."

"But isn't that awkward?"

"It's only awkward if you think clarity is awkward. Text Jordan and say something like: 'Hey, just to clarify, is Saturday a study session or are you asking me on a date? I'm interested either way, but I want to make sure I'm understanding correctly.'"

"I can just... ask directly?"

"Autistic people can and should ask directly. It's actually one of our strengths. We're honest and clear about what we want and need. That's valuable, especially in relationships."

Aria pulled out her phone and typed: *Hey Jordan, quick question - is Saturday a study date or a date-date? I'm interested in you either way, but I want to make sure I'm reading this right because I'm autistic and I sometimes miss social cues.*

She hit send before she could overthink it.

Jordan replied within minutes: *Haha I was hoping it was a date-date, but I wasn't sure if you were interested. I'm glad you asked directly! Yes, I'm asking you on a date. We can study too if you want, but mainly I just want to hang out with you.*

Aria stared at her phone, feeling a mix of excitement and terror. "Maya, she said yes. Now what do I do?"

"Now you go on a date. And you get to figure out what dating looks like for an autistic person, which might be different from neurotypical dating."

SATURDAY ARRIVED. Aria had spent the week researching "how to date" online, which had mostly yielded contradictory advice and made her more anxious.

Jordan arrived at 2 PM exactly. Aria had cleaned her room, prepared physics study materials just in case, and made a list of conversation topics in case she ran out of things to say.

"Hey!" Jordan said with a warm smile. "Nice room. Are those model rockets?"

"Yes, I built them. They're scale models of various space missions. That one's the Saturn V from Apollo 11, that's Falcon Heavy, and that's —" Aria cut herself off. "Sorry, I'm info dumping about rockets."

"Don't apologize, that's cool! Can you tell me about them?"

Aria hesitated. "Do you actually want to hear about them, or are you just being polite?"

Jordan looked surprised by the question, then thoughtful. "I actually want to hear about them. I like how passionate you get about things."

"Okay, but tell me if I'm talking too much. I don't always notice."

"Deal."

Aria relaxed slightly and explained her rocket collection. Jordan asked questions that seemed genuinely interested. After twenty minutes, Jordan said, "We should probably do some physics studying too, right?"

They settled at Aria's desk with their textbooks. But studying quickly became talking, which became laughing, which became a really nice afternoon.

At some point, Jordan said, "Can I ask you something?"

"Sure."

"You mentioned you're autistic. Can you tell me what that means for you? Like, what's helpful for me to know?"

Aria blinked. No one had ever just... asked her that directly before.

"Um. I'm very literal, so I miss sarcasm and implied meanings sometimes. I need people to be direct about what they want instead of hinting. I don't always make eye contact because it's uncomfortable. Sometimes I need breaks from socializing because it's exhausting to process everything. I have strong opinions and I express them honestly, which people sometimes think is rude but I'm not trying to be rude."

"Okay, that's all really helpful to know. What else?"

"I stim sometimes—I have a fidget cube I use. Loud environments are overwhelming. I like having schedules and knowing what to expect. And I'm probably going to accidentally do or say things that are weird or socially wrong because I don't always know the rules."

"Okay. Here's what would be helpful for me: if I do something that bothers you, just tell me directly. Don't expect me to guess. And if I do something that seems like I'm upset or hinting at something, I'll try to remember to be direct instead. Does that work?"

Aria felt something tight in her chest loosen. "Yes. That works really well."

"Cool. So, I'm going to be direct now: I really like you, and I'd like to keep hanging out like this. Are you interested in dating?"

"Yes," Aria said, appreciating the clarity. "I'm interested. But I should warn you that I've never dated anyone before and I don't really know how it works."

"That's okay. I've dated a few people, but every relationship is different anyway. We can figure out what works for us."

DATING JORDAN TURNED out to be surprisingly manageable when both people communicated directly. Jordan would say "I'd like to hold your hand, is that okay?" instead of just reaching for Aria's hand and expecting her to understand the gesture. Aria would say "I need to go home now because I'm getting overstimulated" instead of forcing herself to endure uncomfortable situations.

But there were still moments where Aria misstepped.

Two weeks into dating, they were at a movie with a group of friends. Jordan mentioned feeling cold, and Aria said, "You should have brought a jacket. The theater is always cold."

Jordan got quiet. Later, when they were alone, Jordan said, "I felt hurt when you said that about the jacket."

"What? I was just stating a fact."

"I know. But when I said I was cold, I was kind of hinting that I wanted you to offer me your jacket, or put your arm around me, or something romantic like that."

"Oh." Aria processed this. "I don't understand hints. You said you'd be direct."

"You're right, I'm sorry. I fell back into neurotypical communication patterns. Let me be clear: when I'm cold at the movies, I'd like you to offer your jacket or cuddle with me for warmth."

"Okay, I can do that. But Jordan, I'm not going to pick up on hints. Ever. My brain doesn't work that way. So we need to agree that you'll always say what you mean directly, especially about emotional or romantic stuff."

"Deal. And I need to know: is there stuff I'm doing that bothers you but you're not saying?"

Aria thought about it. "Sometimes you touch me unexpectedly and it startles me. Like when you grab my arm to get my attention. It would be better if you said my name first, or tapped my shoulder gently."

"Okay, I'll do that. See? This is good. We're learning each other's communication styles."

DESPITE THEIR BEST efforts at direct communication, misunderstandings still happened.

One day at lunch, Jordan's friend Emma was talking about a difficult situation with her parents. Aria listened, then offered advice:

"You should tell your parents directly what you need instead of expecting them to guess. Also, you're partially at fault here because you didn't communicate your boundaries clearly earlier."

Emma's face fell. She got up and left the table.

Jordan turned to Aria. "That was kind of harsh."

"What? She was describing a problem. I offered a solution."

"She wasn't looking for solutions. She wanted empathy and support."

"But solving the problem would help her feel better."

"Maybe, but timing matters. When someone's upset, they usually need emotional support first, and problem-solving second. Sometimes they don't want problem-solving at all—they just want to be heard."

Aria felt frustrated. "How am I supposed to know which one someone wants?"

"Usually you can ask. Say something like 'Do you want advice, or do you want me to listen?'"

Aria added this to her guide under a new section: **EMOTIONAL SUPPORT RULES - Ask if they want advice or just listening. Don't jump straight to problem-solving.**

Later, Aria found Emma and apologized.

"I'm sorry for what I said at lunch. Jordan helped me understand that you were looking for emotional support, not solutions. I'm autistic and I sometimes miss that distinction. I was trying to be helpful but I realize I came across as insensitive."

Emma looked surprised. "Oh. I didn't know you were autistic. That makes more sense. I thought you were just being kind of mean."

"I wasn't trying to be mean. I genuinely thought offering solutions was helping."

"I appreciate you explaining that. And honestly, your advice wasn't wrong. I do need to communicate better with my parents. I just wasn't ready to hear it in that moment."

. . .

As Aria's relationship with Jordan deepened, she realized that dating as an autistic person meant constantly navigating two worlds: the direct, logical communication that felt natural, and the subtle, emotion-based communication that neurotypical people expected.

Some things Jordan did that seemed romantic to her just confused Aria. Surprise dates made Aria anxious because she couldn't prepare. Flowers seemed impractical—why give someone plants that would die? Metaphorical love language made no sense.

But other things worked beautifully. When Jordan said "I love spending time with you" instead of playing it cool, Aria felt secure in the relationship. When they made specific plans instead of vague "we should hang out" statements, Aria knew exactly what to expect. When Jordan asked "Are you okay?" and actually wanted to know instead of just being polite, Aria felt seen.

One evening, three months into dating, they had a conversation about their future.

"Do you think this is going to work long-term?" Jordan asked. "Like, doesn't it bother you that you have to work so hard to translate my neurotypical communication?"

"Sometimes," Aria admitted. "But you're also working to communicate more directly for me. It's not one-sided."

"I just worry that I'm going to accidentally hurt you by being indirect, or you're going to accidentally hurt me by being too blunt."

"That's probably going to happen sometimes," Aria said. "But we're both trying. And honestly, I'd rather be with someone who communicates honestly and directly, even if I have to explicitly ask for that, than with someone who expects me to read their mind and gets mad when I can't."

"That's fair. I actually really like your directness. My last relationship ended partly because we never said what we actually meant. Everything was hints and games and unexpressed expectations. This is so much clearer."

"Really? Neurotypical people like directness?"

"Some of us do. I think a lot of the 'neurotypical communication style' stuff is actually just bad communication that's been normalized.

Like, why would anyone prefer hinting over clear statements? That's just inefficient and prone to misunderstanding."

Aria laughed. "I've been saying that for years."

AT SCHOOL, Aria's social translation guide had grown to over twenty pages. She'd documented patterns in greetings, compliments, criticism, emotional support, romantic gestures, and countless other social situations.

Her friend Riley asked to see it one day.

"Wow, this is comprehensive," Riley said. "You've basically created a neurotypical-to-autistic dictionary."

"It helps. Although new situations keep coming up that I haven't documented yet."

"Can I show this to my cousin? He's autistic and he struggles with similar stuff."

"Sure. Actually..." Aria had an idea. "What if I made this into a resource other autistic people could use? Like, a crowdsourced guide where people add the social rules they've figured out?"

Riley's eyes lit up. "That would be amazing. There are probably thousands of autistic teens who need exactly this."

With help from Riley and Maya, Aria created an online document where autistic people could share decoded social rules, confusing situations they'd navigated, and strategies that worked for them. Within weeks, dozens of people had contributed.

Reading other autistic people's experiences made Aria feel less alone. She wasn't the only one who found neurotypical communication exhausting and illogical. She wasn't weird for needing explicit instructions about social rules that others seemed to absorb automatically.

And reading about others' successes—autistic people who'd built good friendships, started relationships, navigated workplace communication—gave Aria hope that she could figure this out too.

· · ·

By the end of junior year, Aria had developed what Maya called "practical social fluency." She still didn't intuitively understand neurotypical social scripts, but she'd learned enough patterns to avoid the worst misunderstandings. She'd also gotten much better at recognizing when she needed clarification and actually asking for it.

More importantly, Aria had built a social circle that worked for her: Jordan, who valued direct communication; Riley, who patiently explained confusing social situations; a few other neurodivergent friends who shared her communication style; and even some neurotypical friends who'd learned to be more explicit in their communication.

"You know what I realized?" Aria told Maya during one of their regular check-ins. "I spent so much time trying to figure out neurotypical communication that I didn't appreciate the strengths of autistic communication."

"Like what?"

"Like honesty. Efficiency. Saying what we mean. Asking for what we need. Those are actually really valuable traits, especially in relationships. Jordan says our relationship works better than her previous ones partly because we're so clear with each other."

"That's a good realization. You don't have to become neurotypical to have good relationships. You just have to find people who value your communication style, and learn enough about neurotypical patterns to avoid major misunderstandings."

"And to help neurotypical people understand my style too. Like, I tell people upfront now that I'm autistic and I need direct communication. If they can't handle that, they're not my people."

"Exactly. The right people will meet you halfway."

At prom that spring, Jordan and Aria had negotiated exactly how the evening would work: arrive at 7, stay until 9:30, take breaks in the quiet hallway when Aria needed them, leave together before the after-parties that would be too overwhelming.

During a slow song, Jordan pulled Aria close and said, "I'm really glad we're together."

"Me too."

"Even though dating me means dealing with my neurotypical weirdness?"

"Even though. You're worth the translation effort."

Jordan laughed. "You're so romantic."

"I'm being literal."

"I know. That's what I love about you."

Aria smiled. She still didn't always understand neurotypical social scripts. She still made mistakes and had awkward moments. But she'd learned that being autistic didn't mean she couldn't have meaningful friendships and relationships—it just meant she needed to find people who appreciated honesty over hints, clarity over games, and authenticity over performance.

And she had.

~

REFLECT

1. What social rules or expectations do you find confusing or exhausting?

Think about the "unwritten rules" that everyone else seems to know but you don't. What social situations leave you feeling confused about what you did wrong? What aspects of communication feel like you're missing the instructions?

____

____

____

____

____

2. Have you ever been told you're "too blunt," "too honest," or "too direct"? How did that feel?

Consider the times when your straightforward communication style has been criticized. Were you actually being rude, or were you just not following neurotypical indirect communication patterns?

____

____

____

____

____

3. Do you spend a lot of energy trying to figure out what people "really mean" vs. what they actually say?

Reflect on the mental exhaustion of translating indirect communication. How much time and energy do you spend trying to decode hints, implications, and subtext?

____

____

____

____

____

4. In your relationships (friendships or romantic), do you feel comfortable asking for direct communication?

Think about whether you feel safe saying "I need you to be explicit about what you want" or "I don't understand hints, please tell me directly." What happens when you make these requests?

____

____

____

____

____

5. What strengths does your direct communication style offer?

Consider the positive aspects of autistic communication: honesty, clarity, efficiency, authenticity. How might these traits be valuable in relationships, even if they're different from neurotypical norms?

____

____

____

____

____

~

ACT

This week, create your own "social translation guide" and practice asking for direct communication in at least one relationship.

Step 1: Start your social translation guide

Create a document (digital or physical) where you'll record confusing social situations and decoded rules. Use Aria's format or create your own:

Template:

- **Situation:** What happened
- **My interpretation:** What I thought was going on
- **Actual social rule:** What I was supposed to understand
- **How to handle next time:** Strategy for similar situations

Example:

- **Situation:** Friend asked "how do I look?" before a date
- **My interpretation:** They wanted honest feedback on their outfit
- **Actual social rule:** They wanted reassurance and compliments, not critique
- **How to handle next time:** Always start with compliments ("You look great!") unless they specifically ask "what should I change?"

Step 2: Document 3-5 past confusing interactions
Think back to times when:

- Someone got upset and you didn't understand why
- You said something and people reacted unexpectedly
- You missed a social cue that others apparently caught
- Someone accused you of being rude when you thought
  you were being helpful

Write these down and try to decode what you missed. If you're not sure, ask someone you trust to help translate.

Step 3: Identify one person who you can ask for "translation help"
Find someone who:

- Is patient and willing to explain social situations
- Knows you're autistic/neurodivergent
- Won't judge you for needing clarification
- Can explain unwritten rules explicitly

Ask them: "Can I check in with you when I have confusing social situations? I'm trying to build a better understanding of social expectations, and it helps to have someone explain what I'm missing."

Step 4: Practice asking for direct communication
Choose one relationship (friend, family member, romantic partner) where you want clearer communication. Have a conversation:

"I want to tell you something about how I communicate. I'm [autistic/neurodivergent] and I don't pick up on hints or indirect communication well. It would really help me if you could:

- *Say what you mean directly instead of hinting*
- *Tell me explicitly if you want advice or just listening when you're upset*
- *Let me know if I've said something that hurt you, because I might not realize*

- *Ask me directly for what you need instead of expecting me to guess*

I'm not asking you to change your whole communication style, but in our relationship specifically, more directness would help me understand you better and avoid accidental hurt."

Step 5: In one social situation this week, ask a clarifying question instead of guessing

When you're confused about:

- What someone meant
- What someone wants from you
- Whether you've made a social mistake
- What the "right" response is

Instead of guessing or stressing, practice asking:

- "I want to make sure I understand—are you asking for advice or do you want me to just listen?"
- "When you say [thing], do you mean [interpretation]?"
- "I'm not sure how to respond to that. Can you be more specific about what you need?"
- "Did I say something wrong just now? I can't tell and I want to understand."

Step 6: Notice when YOUR communication style is actually BETTER

Pay attention to situations where your directness, honesty, or clarity is actually more effective than neurotypical indirect communication. Document these wins:

- Times when your honest feedback helped someone
- Situations where your clear communication prevented misunderstanding

- Relationships that improved because you asked for what you needed
- Moments when someone appreciated your straightforwardness

Step 7: Reflect on the experience
At the end of the week:

- How does it feel to document social rules explicitly?
- Did asking for direct communication improve any relationships?
- What social patterns are you starting to recognize?
- How did people respond when you asked clarifying questions?
- What strengths of your communication style did you notice?

Important reminders:

- You're not "bad at communication"—you have a different communication style
- Neurotypical indirect communication isn't superior—it's just more common
- You deserve relationships where people say what they mean
- Asking for clarification is not rude—it's honest
- Your direct communication style has real value
- The right people will meet you halfway

Extension challenge:
If you're comfortable, share your social translation guide with other autistic/neurodivergent people. You might:

- Post it in an online neurodivergent community
- Share it with autistic friends or family members

- Contribute to existing resources about autistic social navigation

Your decoded social rules might help someone else who's struggling with the same confusing situations. And reading others' guides will help you recognize patterns faster.

Remember: Learning neurotypical social scripts is a practical survival skill, but it doesn't mean your communication style is wrong. The goal isn't to become neurotypical—it's to build enough fluency to navigate neurotypical spaces while finding people who appreciate your authentic communication style.

8

———

THE DIAGNOSIS MOMENT

Sofia sat in Dr. Patel's office, staring at the assessment report in her hands. The words seemed to swim on the page, but one phrase stood out in bold: **Diagnosis: Attention-Deficit/Hyperactivity Disorder (ADHD), Predominantly Inattentive Presentation.**

"So... I have ADHD," Sofia said slowly, testing the words out loud.

"Yes," Dr. Patel confirmed gently. "The testing shows a clear pattern of ADHD symptoms that have significantly impacted your academic performance and daily functioning."

Sofia felt something crack open inside her chest—not breaking, but opening. Like a door she'd been pushing against for years had suddenly swung wide.

She was sixteen years old, and for the first time in her life, she had an explanation for why everything felt so hard.

THREE MONTHS **earlier**

Sofia had always thought of herself as lazy. Unmotivated. Lacking willpower. Those were the words teachers used in parent conferences, the labels her parents threw around when she forgot assignments or zoned out during conversations.

"If you just applied yourself..." "You're so smart, if you would only try..." "Why can't you just focus?"

Sofia had heard these phrases so many times they'd become her internal monologue. When she couldn't start homework until the night before it was due, she told herself she was procrastinating by choice. When she lost track of time and showed up late, she blamed herself for being inconsiderate. When she forgot important information her parents had told her three times, she called herself stupid.

The breaking point came during a college planning meeting with her school counselor.

"Your test scores are excellent, Sofia," Ms. Chen said, reviewing her file. "Your teachers say you're clearly intelligent and engaged in class discussions. But your GPA is only 2.8 because of missing assignments and inconsistent performance. That's going to limit your college options significantly."

"I know," Sofia said, feeling the familiar weight of shame. "I'm working on being more organized."

"You've been 'working on it' since freshman year," Ms. Chen pointed out, not unkindly. "And the pattern hasn't changed. That suggests to me that this might not be a motivation issue."

Sofia looked up. "What do you mean?"

"I mean that students who are intelligent and want to succeed but consistently struggle with organization, time management, and task completion despite trying hard... sometimes there's an underlying reason beyond just needing to try harder."

"Like what?"

"Like ADHD, or executive function difficulties, or other neurodevelopmental conditions that affect those skills." Ms. Chen pulled out a screening questionnaire. "Would you be willing to fill this out? It's not a diagnosis, but it might help us understand what's going on."

.   .   .

SOFIA HAD ALWAYS THOUGHT ADHD meant hyperactive boys who couldn't sit still. She wasn't hyperactive. She could sit for hours—usually hyperfocusing on her phone or a book while completely losing track of homework she was supposed to be doing.

But as she filled out the questionnaire, question after question hit uncomfortably close to home:

Do you have difficulty sustaining attention in tasks? Yes. Constantly.

Do you often fail to give close attention to details or make careless mistakes? Every single assignment.

Do you have difficulty organizing tasks and activities? Her backpack was a disaster zone and her room looked like a tornado hit it.

Do you avoid tasks that require sustained mental effort? She'd been putting off a history paper for three weeks.

Do you often lose things necessary for tasks? She'd lost four calculators this year alone.

Are you easily distracted by external stimuli? A bird outside the window could derail her entire focus.

Are you forgetful in daily activities? She forgot her lunch, her homework, conversations, appointments, everything.

By the end of the questionnaire, Sofia felt exposed. It was like someone had been watching her struggle for sixteen years and written down everything she thought was her personal failing.

Ms. Chen reviewed her responses and said gently, "Sofia, I think you should talk to your parents about getting a comprehensive ADHD evaluation."

HER PARENTS WERE SKEPTICAL.

"ADHD is overdiagnosed these days," her dad said. "Everyone wants a label for normal teenage behavior."

"I don't think this is normal," Sofia argued. "I've been struggling with this stuff my entire life. It's not just teenage laziness."

"You just need better time management skills," her mom said. "Maybe we should take your phone away so you're less distracted."

"Taking my phone away won't help me remember where I put my

homework, or make my brain stop wandering during lectures, or help me start tasks that feel overwhelming."

Her parents looked at each other—that silent conversation married couples have.

"If we do this evaluation," her dad finally said, "and it comes back saying you don't have ADHD, will you accept that you just need to work harder at organization?"

Sofia wanted to scream. But she said, "If I don't have ADHD, then we can figure out what else is going on. Because something is going on. I'm not choosing to fail. I'm trying as hard as I can and it's still not enough."

Something in her voice must have gotten through, because her mom's expression softened.

"Okay," she said. "We'll make an appointment."

THE EVALUATION PROCESS

The ADHD evaluation took weeks. Sofia met with Dr. Patel three times for interviews, filled out questionnaires, and did computer-based attention tests. Her parents and teachers filled out their own questionnaires about Sofia's behavior and performance.

The waiting was excruciating. Sofia swung between hope that she'd finally have answers and fear that the tests would come back "normal" and she'd be back to believing she was just lazy and undisciplined.

During the evaluation, Dr. Patel asked questions that made Sofia's struggles feel seen in a way they never had before:

"Do you often start tasks but struggle to finish them?" "Do you hyperfocus on things that interest you but can't sustain attention on things that don't?" "Do you experience time blindness—losing track of how much time has passed?" "Do you have intense emotional reactions to criticism or perceived rejection?"

That last question hit Sofia hard.

"Yes," she admitted. "I've always been really sensitive to criticism. Like, someone can give me 90% positive feedback and 10% constructive criticism, and I'll fixate on the critical part for days. My friends say I overreact to small things."

"Can you give me an example?"

"Last week, my friend Mia was busy and couldn't hang out. She said 'sorry, I have plans.' But my brain immediately went to 'she doesn't actually want to hang out with me, she's making an excuse, she's pulling away from our friendship.' I spent two days convinced she hated me, even though logically I knew she was just busy."

"That emotional intensity in response to perceived rejection is actually common in ADHD. It's sometimes called Rejection Sensitive Dysphoria. Your emotional regulation is affected by the same neurotransmitter issues that affect your attention and executive function."

Sofia felt tears prick her eyes. There was a name for it. A reason. It wasn't just her being overly dramatic or emotionally unstable.

THE DIAGNOSIS MOMENT

Now, sitting in Dr. Patel's office with the official diagnosis in her hands, Sofia felt a complicated tangle of emotions.

Relief. Finally, an explanation for why everything was so hard.

Validation. She wasn't lazy or stupid. Her brain literally worked differently.

Anger. Why had no one noticed this before? Why had she spent sixteen years thinking she was fundamentally flawed?

Grief. For all the times she'd struggled unnecessarily. For the GPA she could have had if she'd been diagnosed and treated earlier. For the self-esteem damage from years of being told to "just try harder."

Hope. Maybe things could get better now. Maybe she could actually function like she'd always wanted to.

"How are you feeling?" Dr. Patel asked.

"I don't know," Sofia said honestly. "A lot of things at once."

"That's very normal. Getting diagnosed as a teenager, especially for girls with inattentive ADHD, often comes with complex emotions. You've spent years developing an identity around struggling, and now you're learning that the struggle had a neurological basis."

"I'm mad that no one caught this earlier," Sofia admitted. "Why didn't my teachers notice? Why didn't my parents notice?"

"ADHD in girls, especially inattentive presentation, is significantly underdiagnosed. You weren't hyperactive or disruptive. You were quiet, daydreaming, struggling internally. That often gets missed because it doesn't cause problems for others—only for you."

"So I've just been suffering alone this whole time?"

"Unfortunately, yes. But now that we know what's going on, we can address it. There are medications that can help, behavioral strategies you can learn, accommodations you can get at school. This diagnosis opens doors."

SOFIA LEFT the appointment with prescriptions, referrals, and educational materials about ADHD. She sat in her car for twenty minutes, staring at the diagnosis paperwork, processing everything.

Her phone buzzed. A text from her best friend Lily: *How'd the appointment go?*

Sofia took a photo of the diagnosis page and sent it: *I have ADHD.*

Holy shit! How do you feel?

Relieved? Angry? Sad? All of it?

That's fair. Want to talk about it?

Not yet. I need to process first.

Okay. I'm here when you're ready. Love you.

Sofia appreciated that Lily didn't push. She needed time to sit with this new understanding of herself.

THAT EVENING, Sofia told her parents.

"The results came back. I have ADHD."

Her mom looked upset in a way Sofia couldn't quite read. "Are you sure? Did they do thorough testing?"

"Yes, Mom. Comprehensive evaluation. Multiple sessions. Questionnaires from you, from my teachers. Computer tests. It's ADHD."

"So what does that mean?" her dad asked.

"It means all the things you thought were character flaws—my disorganization, my forgetfulness, my inability to start homework until the last minute—those are symptoms of a neurological condition. It means my brain produces less dopamine and norepinephrine than typical brains, which affects my executive function, attention, and emotional regulation."

Her parents were quiet.

"It also means," Sofia continued, feeling anger rise in her voice, "that every time you told me I just needed to try harder, you were asking me to fix a neurological condition through willpower. Which is like telling someone with bad eyesight to just try harder to see."

"Sofia—" her mom started.

"No, let me finish. I've spent years thinking I was lazy and stupid. I've hated myself for not being able to do things that seemed easy for everyone else. And now I find out there was actually a reason, and no one noticed. No one helped me. I just struggled alone while everyone told me to apply myself more."

Her mom's eyes filled with tears. "We didn't know. If we had known—"

"But you should have known! The signs were all there! I was obviously struggling! But instead of thinking 'maybe something else is going on,' you just assumed I wasn't trying hard enough!"

Sofia was crying now, years of frustration and shame pouring out.

Her dad stood up and pulled her into a hug. She tried to resist, still angry, but eventually collapsed into it.

"You're right," he said quietly. "We should have seen it. We should have looked deeper instead of just pushing you to do better. I'm sorry."

"I'm so sorry," her mom echoed, joining the hug. "We thought we were motivating you. We didn't realize we were making you feel worse about something you couldn't control."

They stood there for a long time, Sofia crying out years of accumulated pain while her parents held her and apologized.

. . .

PROCESSING **the diagnosis**

Over the next few weeks, Sofia went through stages of processing what the diagnosis meant.

Week 1: Research phase

Sofia consumed everything she could find about ADHD. She watched YouTube videos by adults with ADHD, read articles, joined online communities. Each new piece of information was another "oh my god, that's me" moment.

Time blindness. Emotional dysregulation. Hyperfixation. Object permanence issues. Rejection Sensitive Dysphoria. Difficulty with task initiation. Working memory challenges. All of it described her experiences with painful accuracy.

She started reframing her entire life through the lens of ADHD:

That time in middle school when I forgot my best friend's birthday party and she thought I didn't care? ADHD working memory problems, not me being a bad friend.

All those times I started projects with enthusiasm and never finished them? ADHD difficulty with sustained attention and task completion, not me being flaky.

The way I'd get irrationally upset when someone criticized me? Rejection Sensitive Dysphoria, not me being overly emotional.

My messy room that I genuinely couldn't seem to organize? ADHD executive function challenges, not me being lazy.

Each reframe was painful and liberating at once—painful because she'd suffered so much unnecessary shame, liberating because she finally understood it wasn't her fault.

Week 2: Anger phase

The anger came in waves. Sofia was furious at:

- Teachers who'd called her lazy instead of recognizing she needed help
- Parents who'd punished her for symptoms she couldn't control
- Doctors who'd never screened her for ADHD during routine checkups

- A system that routinely missed ADHD in girls because they weren't disruptive
- Herself, for all the years she'd believed she was just fundamentally flawed

She wrote long, angry journal entries. She ranted to Lily. She cried frustrated tears in the shower.

"I could have been diagnosed at eight," she told her therapist in their first session post-diagnosis. "I showed signs that early. But no one looked because I was quiet and did okay enough in school. And now I'm sixteen with a terrible GPA and damaged self-esteem because everyone just assumed I wasn't trying."

"Your anger is valid," her therapist said. "You deserved better. It's okay to grieve the support you should have received."

Week 3: Grief phase

The grief hit hardest when Sofia thought about who she might have been with proper support.

She looked at her transcript—the C's and D's in classes she actually understood but couldn't organize herself enough to succeed in. The missed assignments that tanked her grades despite acing tests. The comments from teachers: "bright student but doesn't apply herself."

She thought about the social situations she'd messed up because her ADHD made her interrupt people, or forget important details, or miss social cues when she was distracted. Friendships that had faded because she'd forgotten to respond to texts or follow through on plans.

She thought about the mental health struggles—the anxiety from constantly feeling behind, the depression from thinking she was fundamentally inadequate, the low self-esteem from years of failure.

"I'm mourning a version of myself that never got to exist," she told Lily one afternoon. "The Sofia who got diagnosed at eight and grew up with proper support and accommodations. That Sofia probably has a 4.0 and healthy self-esteem and didn't spend her teenage years hating herself."

"You can't change the past," Lily said gently. "But you can change the future. You know now. You can get help now."

Week 4: Hope phase

Slowly, the hope started to outweigh the anger and grief.

Sofia started medication, and the difference was dramatic. Within days, she could:

- Start homework without two hours of paralyzed avoidance first
- Sustain attention through an entire class lecture
- Remember what she walked into a room for
- Control her impulses to interrupt or hyperfocus

"Is this how neurotypical people feel all the time?" she asked her mom in wonder after her first week on medication. "Like, you just... decide to do something and then you do it?"

Her mom laughed despite the tears in her eyes. "I think so, honey."

"That's wild. I've been operating on hard mode my entire life."

Sofia also started learning ADHD-specific strategies:

- Breaking tasks into tiny steps instead of looking at the overwhelming whole
- Using timers and alarms to combat time blindness
- Creating external structures since her internal executive function was unreliable
- Asking for accommodations at school (extended time, copies of notes, quiet testing environments)

For the first time in her life, Sofia felt like she was working with her brain instead of constantly fighting against it.

The **RSD** revelation

One of the most life-changing aspects of the diagnosis was understanding Rejection Sensitive Dysphoria.

Sofia had always experienced criticism and rejection as almost physically painful. A casual comment from a teacher could ruin her entire day. A friend canceling plans felt like a personal attack. Any hint of disappointment from her parents triggered intense shame spirals.

She'd thought she was just too sensitive, too emotional, too fragile. Learning that RSD was a neurological feature of ADHD—that her emotional pain was real and disproportionate because of how her brain processed social feedback—changed everything.

"So when my coach said my performance was 'fine' and I spent three days convinced she hated me and I should quit the team... that was RSD?" Sofia asked Dr. Patel.

"That's a classic RSD response. 'Fine' felt like crushing criticism because your ADHD brain amplified the perceived negative feedback."

"And when my mom said she was 'a little disappointed' about my grade and I had a complete meltdown?"

"Also RSD. Your emotional response was disproportionate to the actual stimulus, but the pain you felt was very real."

Understanding RSD didn't make the pain go away, but it gave Sofia tools to manage it:

- Recognizing when her emotional response was disproportionate to the situation
- Pausing before reacting to perceived criticism
- Asking for clarification when her brain interpreted something as rejection
- Reminding herself that RSD was distorting her perception

When her friend Emma was short with her one day, Sofia's immediate thought was: *She's mad at me. I did something wrong. She doesn't want to be friends anymore.*

But instead of spiraling, Sofia texted: *Hey, are we okay? My brain is telling me you're upset with me, but I want to check if that's real or if I'm misreading things.*

Emma responded immediately: *Oh my god, I'm not upset at you at all! I'm just stressed about my calc test. Sorry if I seemed off.*

That one interaction—checking the reality instead of assuming the worst—prevented a three-day anxiety spiral. Sofia felt powerful.

Telling people

Deciding who to tell about her diagnosis was complicated.

Some people were supportive. Lily said, "This makes so much sense! I'm glad you finally have answers." Her favorite teacher, Mr. Rodriguez, shared that he also had ADHD and offered to help her navigate accommodations.

But others were... less helpful.

"ADHD isn't real, everyone's a little distracted sometimes," one classmate said dismissively.

"You just need more discipline," an aunt told her at a family dinner.

"Are you sure you're not just using this as an excuse?" a friend asked.

Each dismissive comment triggered Sofia's RSD hard. She wanted to scream, to explain, to make them understand. But she was learning to pick her battles.

"I'm not interested in debating the validity of my diagnosis," she started saying to skeptics. "I've been comprehensively evaluated by a medical professional. You're entitled to your opinion, but I'm not going to defend my neurology to you."

It felt good to advocate for herself instead of absorbing others' ignorance.

Six months later

Sofia sat in Ms. Chen's office for a follow-up college planning meeting.

"Your GPA has jumped from 2.8 to 3.4 this semester," Ms. Chen said, smiling. "That's remarkable progress."

"Turns out treating my ADHD and getting accommodations helps a lot," Sofia said, allowing herself to feel proud.

"How are you feeling about college applications now?"

"Better. I'm going to write my personal statement about getting diagnosed with ADHD. About how I spent years thinking I was lazy and undisciplined, and how understanding my neurodivergence changed everything."

"That could be a powerful essay."

"I think it will be. Because lots of colleges say they value diversity and overcoming obstacles. Well, I've spent sixteen years overcoming the obstacle of undiagnosed ADHD in a system that wasn't designed for neurodivergent brains. That's worth something."

SOFIA'S DIAGNOSIS didn't fix everything. She still struggled with organization, time management, and emotional regulation. She still had bad ADHD days where nothing worked right. She still dealt with RSD spirals and executive function fails.

But she had context now. Understanding. Tools. Support. Accommodations. Self-compassion.

Most importantly, she knew the truth: She wasn't lazy. She wasn't stupid. She wasn't broken.

She was neurodivergent. And with proper support, she could thrive.

That knowledge—that fundamental reframe of her entire identity—made all the difference.

REFLECT

1. If you have a diagnosis, what emotions came up when you first learned about it?

Were you relieved? Angry? Grieving? Confused? Validated? All of the above? There's no "right" way to feel about a diagnosis. All your emotions are valid.

____

____

____

____

____

2. If you don't have a diagnosis but suspect you might be neurodivergent, what's stopping you from seeking evaluation?

Is it access to healthcare? Fear of what you might learn? Skeptical parents? Concern about labels? Identify the barriers so you can start addressing them.

____

____

____

____

____

3. How has your neurodivergence (diagnosed or suspected) been explained to you?

Were you told it's a "difference," a "disorder," a "disability," a "challenge," or something else? How do those different framings affect how you see yourself?

____

____

____

____

____

4. What would change in your life if you had clear answers about how your brain works?

Think about the accommodations you could request, the self-compassion you could develop, the strategies you could implement. How might diagnosis or deeper understanding shift your trajectory?

____

____

____

____

____

5. Are you grieving a version of yourself that could have existed with earlier support?

This grief is real and valid. Many late-diagnosed neurodivergent people mourn the struggles they endured unnecessarily. How can you honor that grief while also focusing on the future?

____

____

____

____

____

〜

ACT

This week, work toward better understanding your neurodivergence—whether that means pursuing diagnosis, learning about your existing diagnosis, or just gaining clarity about how your brain works.

Step 1: If you suspect you're neurodivergent but undiagnosed, take the first concrete step toward evaluation

This might look like:

- Taking a screening questionnaire online (ADHD, autism, dyslexia, etc.) - these aren't diagnoses but can indicate if evaluation is warranted

- Talking to your school counselor about evaluation resources
- Asking your parents to schedule an appointment with your doctor to discuss concerns
- Researching what evaluation involves so it feels less scary
- Connecting with your school's special education department about evaluation options

If your parents are resistant: Prepare what you'll say:

- "I'm not looking for an excuse or a label. I'm looking for answers about why I struggle with [specific things] despite trying really hard."
- "Evaluation doesn't mean I'll automatically be diagnosed with anything. It's just gathering information."
- "If nothing's wrong, great. But if there is something going on, earlier identification means earlier support."
- Show them the screening questionnaire you filled out and explain why so many questions resonated

Step 2: If you're recently diagnosed, give yourself permission to feel ALL the emotions

Create space to process by:

- Journaling about your diagnosis experience and the emotions that come up
- Talking to someone who understands (therapist, support group, online community)
- Making a list of things you can reframe through your diagnosis (times you blamed yourself for symptoms you couldn't control)
- Allowing yourself to be angry about late diagnosis or lack of support
- Giving yourself permission to grieve while also holding hope for the future

Step 3: Learn about your specific neurodivergence from actually neurodivergent sources

Research your diagnosis (or suspected neurodivergence) by:

- Finding YouTube channels run BY neurodivergent people (not just about them)
- Joining online communities (Reddit, Discord, TikTok) where neurodivergent people share experiences
- Reading books written by neurodivergent authors
- Following neurodivergent advocates on social media
- Distinguishing between medical model explanations (deficit-focused) and neurodiversity model explanations (difference-focused)

Why this matters: Clinical descriptions of ADHD, autism, dyslexia, etc. are often written by neurotypical people and focus on deficits. Neurodivergent people's own descriptions focus on lived experience and strengths.

Step 4: Make a list of things that now make sense

Write down experiences you can now reframe through your diagnosis:

Before diagnosis: I thought I was lazy Now: I understand that task initiation is an executive function challenge related to ADHD

Before diagnosis: I thought I was oversensitive Now: I understand that Rejection Sensitive Dysphoria is a neurological feature of ADHD

Before diagnosis: I thought I was rude for interrupting Now: I understand that impulse control is affected by my ADHD

This reframing isn't about excusing problematic behaviors—it's about replacing shame with understanding so you can develop appropriate strategies.

Step 5: Identify one accommodation or strategy you can implement immediately

Based on your diagnosis (or suspected neurodivergence), choose ONE support to try this week:

- Request extended time on tests
- Start using a timer to combat time blindness
- Ask for written instructions when verbal ones get lost
- Use noise-canceling headphones in overwhelming environments
- Break large tasks into tiny steps
- Set up external organization systems
- Request copies of class notes
- Use assistive technology (text-to-speech, speech-to-text, etc.)

Start with ONE thing. Build from there.

Step 6: Practice self-compassion

When you struggle with something related to your neurodivergence, practice reframing:

Instead of: *"I'm so stupid, why can't I just remember things?"* Try: *"My working memory is affected by ADHD. This is a symptom, not a character flaw. What accommodation could help?"*

Instead of: *"I'm so weird and socially awkward."* Try: *"I'm autistic and process social information differently. That's not wrong, it's just different."*

Instead of: *"Everyone else can do this easily, what's wrong with me?"* Try: *"This task is easier for neurotypical brains. It's okay that I need a different approach or more time."*

Step 7: Connect with one other person who shares your neurodivergence

Find community:

- Online forums or Discord servers for your specific diagnosis
- School clubs or support groups for neurodivergent students
- Local meetups (check libraries, community centers)
- Reach out to someone you know who shares your diagnosis

Connection with people who "get it" without explanation is powerful medicine for the isolation many neurodivergent people feel.

Step 8: If you're experiencing grief about late diagnosis, write a letter

Write a letter to:

- Your younger self, acknowledging the struggles they endured
- Your future self, expressing hope about what's possible now
- The people who missed your signs, expressing how their oversight affected you (you don't have to send this)
- Your current self, offering compassion and understanding

Example: *Dear 10-year-old me,*

I'm sorry no one realized you were struggling with more than just "not trying hard enough." I'm sorry you spent so many years thinking you were fundamentally flawed. You weren't. Your brain just works differently, and you deserved support instead of criticism. I'm going to make sure we get that support now.

Love, 16-year-old me

Remember:

- Diagnosis is information, not identity—but it can be identity-affirming
- Late diagnosis is common, especially for girls, POC, and inattentive presentations
- Your struggles were real, even before you had a label for them
- Diagnosis opens doors to accommodations, strategies, community, and self-understanding
- You deserved better support, and it's okay to grieve that while working toward a better future
- Understanding your neurodivergence is the first step toward thriving with it

9

____

THE STIMMING REVOLUTION

Carlos sat perfectly still in English class, every muscle tensed with the effort of not moving. His hands wanted to flap. His leg wanted to bounce. His fingers wanted to snap in the rhythmic pattern that helped him think. But he kept them all locked down, frozen, controlled.

It had been this way since second grade, when his teacher pulled him aside and said, "Carlos, we need to work on your fidgeting. It's distracting to the other students."

Since then, he'd learned to suppress every natural movement his body wanted to make. No hand flapping. No rocking. No humming. No finger tapping. All the movements that helped him regulate, focus, and process information—gone, pushed down, hidden.

By the time the bell rang, Carlos's body felt like a shaken soda bottle about to explode. He walked quickly to the bathroom, locked himself in a stall, and finally let his hands flap rapidly for thirty seconds. The relief was immediate and intense.

Then the guilt came. He was seventeen years old. Too old to be "doing weird hand things" like when he was little. He needed to have more self-control.

Carlos took a deep breath, composed himself, and headed to his next class, ready to spend another hour sitting perfectly still.

AT HOME THAT EVENING, Carlos scrolled through TikTok while half-watching TV—his usual way of keeping his brain occupied enough to prevent the fidgeting urge. A video appeared in his feed: a young adult with the caption "Stimming is not misbehaving."

The person in the video was openly flapping their hands, rocking back and forth, and fidgeting with a textured toy while talking about autism and self-regulation.

"Stimming—self-stimulatory behavior—is how autistic people regulate our nervous systems," the person explained. "Hand flapping, rocking, spinning, vocal stims, whatever helps your body feel regulated. It's not something to suppress. It's communication and self-care."

Carlos watched, transfixed. He'd been diagnosed with autism at age seven, but no one had ever explained stimming as something positive. It had always been framed as a problem behavior to eliminate.

He scrolled through more videos. Autistic adults proudly stimming on camera. People explaining different types of stims and their purposes. Discussions of how suppressing stims leads to burnout and anxiety.

One video hit particularly hard: "Telling autistic people not to stim is like telling them not to breathe. It's a fundamental need, not a choice."

Carlos thought about all the energy he spent every day suppressing his natural movements. The tension headaches. The anxiety. The exhaustion from constant self-monitoring. Was he literally hurting himself by trying to appear "normal"?

THE NEXT DAY AT LUNCH, Carlos sat with his usual group. His friend Ana was talking about the history test, but Carlos was only half-listening. His leg wanted to bounce. His fingers wanted to drum on the table. He kept them still.

"Carlos, are you even listening?" Ana asked.

"Sorry, yeah, what?"

"I asked if you studied for the history test."

"Oh. Yeah, I studied."

His friend Miguel leaned over. "Dude, why do you always sit so still? You look like a statue. It's kind of unnerving."

Carlos felt heat rise to his face. Even when he was successfully suppressing his stims, people noticed something was off.

"I'm just... sitting."

"You're like, aggressively still though. Are you okay?"

"I'm fine."

But he wasn't fine. His whole body was screaming for movement, and the effort of denying it was making it impossible to focus on the conversation.

"I'll be right back," Carlos said abruptly, heading to the bathroom again for his secret stim break.

In the bathroom stall, he flapped his hands, rocked back and forth, and hummed quietly for two minutes. The relief was overwhelming. Why couldn't he just do this all the time? Why did it have to be this shameful secret?

THAT AFTERNOON, Carlos had an appointment with his therapist, Dr. Kim.

"How's school going?" Dr. Kim asked.

"Fine."

"Carlos, I've known you for three years. 'Fine' usually means 'not fine but I don't want to talk about it.' What's actually going on?"

Carlos sighed. "I'm exhausted all the time. Like, physically and mentally drained. And I keep getting tension headaches. And I'm having trouble concentrating even though I'm trying really hard."

"When did this get worse?"

Carlos thought about it. "I don't know, maybe the past year? It feels like the older I get, the harder it is to... function."

"Can you tell me what a typical day looks like for you?"

Carlos walked through his routine: wake up, get ready for school, sit through seven classes, come home, do homework, sleep. Pretty standard.

"And during those seven classes, what's your body doing?"

"Sitting still. Paying attention."

"Are you naturally still, or are you forcing yourself to be still?"

The question hit like a punch. "Forcing myself, I guess."

"For how many hours a day?"

"I don't know. School is like seven hours. Then I have to sit still at dinner with my family. And when I'm doing homework. So... most of the day?"

"Carlos, what happens when you don't force yourself to be still?"

"I... move. My hands flap. I rock. I make sounds. You know, all the autistic stuff I'm supposed to have grown out of."

Dr. Kim leaned forward. "Who told you that you were supposed to grow out of stimming?"

"Everyone? Teachers, my parents, other kids. They all said I needed to learn to sit still and stop fidgeting."

"And how has that been working for you?"

Carlos looked at his hands. "It's exhausting. I'm constantly monitoring every movement, making sure I'm not doing anything weird. But even when I succeed at staying still, I can't focus because all my energy is going toward controlling my body."

"That's because stimming isn't optional for autistic people. It's a regulatory need. When you suppress it, you're fighting against your nervous system all day long. No wonder you're exhausted."

"But people think it's weird."

"Some people do," Dr. Kim acknowledged. "And for many autistic people, learning to mask stims is a survival skill in hostile environments. But the question is: at what cost? And are all environments hostile, or just some?"

Carlos had never thought about it that way. He'd just assumed all environments required him to suppress his stims.

"What would happen if you stimmed in class?" Dr. Kim asked.

"People would stare. Think I'm weird. Make fun of me."

"Have you tested that theory recently, or are you working from childhood experiences?"

Carlos realized he hadn't actually stimmed openly since elementary school. He had no idea how his current classmates would actually respond.

"Let me give you some homework," Dr. Kim said. "Research the neurodivergent pride movement online. Learn about stimming from actually autistic adults. And consider experimenting with allowing yourself to stim in one low-stakes environment."

THAT NIGHT, Carlos fell down a rabbit hole of neurodivergent content creators. He discovered:

- Autistic adults who stimmed openly on camera and talked about it as self-care
- The concept of "stimming pride"—the idea that stims weren't shameful behaviors to hide but natural movements to celebrate
- Research showing that suppressing stims increased anxiety, made focusing harder, and contributed to autistic burnout
- Stories from late-diagnosed autistic adults who'd spent decades masking their stims and developed serious mental health issues as a result
- The distinction between stims that helped (regulatory) and stims that hurt (harmful)—and how the vast majority of stims were helpful

One video explained: "Stimming is your body's way of regulating sensory input, processing emotions, expressing excitement or stress, and maintaining focus. When you suppress stims, you're cutting off your body's natural regulatory system. It's like unplugging your emotional and sensory processing."

Carlos thought about how much energy he spent suppressing movements that were literally trying to help him function. It was like fighting against his own immune system.

He found a video by an autistic college student who explained their journey from stim suppression to stim acceptance:

"I spent years training myself not to stim because I was ashamed. Then I hit autistic burnout so hard I couldn't function at all. In therapy, I had to relearn how to listen to my body's regulatory needs. Now I stim openly—in class, at work, with friends. And yeah, some people stare. But I'd rather be weird and functional than 'normal' and burned out."

Carlos watched the video three times.

THE NEXT DAY AT SCHOOL, Carlos made a decision. He was going to try stimming in English class—just a little bit. Just to see what happened.

He sat in his usual seat, pulled out a small fidget cube he'd found at home, and started quietly clicking it during the lecture.

Within minutes, he noticed he was actually absorbing what the teacher was saying. His brain wasn't splitting its attention between the lecture and suppressing his body's movement needs. He could just... listen and think and process.

His classmate next to him glanced at the fidget cube, but didn't say anything.

Emboldened, Carlos let his leg bounce quietly under his desk. The combination of the fidget toy and the movement made focusing so much easier.

After class, his classmate said, "Hey, where'd you get that fidget cube? I might need one of those."

"Amazon, I think?"

"Cool, thanks."

That was it. No mockery. No staring. Just a practical question.

· · ·

OVER THE NEXT WEEK, Carlos gradually introduced more stimming into his daily routine:

- He used the fidget cube in most of his classes
- He let his leg bounce freely during homework
- He rocked slightly when he was thinking
- He started humming quietly when he was alone
- He allowed his hands to flap when he got excited or stressed

The difference was dramatic. His tension headaches decreased. His anxiety lessened. He could focus better in class. He had more energy at the end of the day.

But he was still hiding the more visible stims—the hand flapping, the full-body rocking, the vocal stims. Those still felt too "obviously autistic" to do publicly.

EVERYTHING CHANGED the day Carlos attended a neurodivergent student meetup that Dr. Kim had recommended.

He walked into the community center room nervously, not sure what to expect. About fifteen teenagers were there, and immediately Carlos noticed something different: people were stimming.

One person was rocking gently in their chair while talking. Another was flapping their hands while listening. Someone else was clicking a pen repeatedly. Another person was wearing headphones and humming.

And nobody cared. Nobody stared. Nobody told anyone to stop.

Carlos felt something loosen in his chest—a tension he'd been carrying for so long he'd stopped noticing it.

The group facilitator, Alex (they/them), welcomed everyone. "For those who are new, this is a space where you can be your authentic neurodivergent self. Stim freely, use whatever accommodations you need, communicate however works for you. The only rule is respecting others' needs and boundaries."

The meeting was a discussion about dealing with sensory overload at school. As people talked, Carlos noticed how much stimming accompanied the conversation. People gestured enthusiastically, rocked, fidgeted with toys, moved constantly.

And it was beautiful. Everyone was so present, so engaged, so clearly comfortable in their bodies.

When it was Carlos's turn to share, he felt nervous energy build up. Instinctively, his hands started to flap.

He caught himself and stopped.

"You can stim here," Alex said gently. "That's what that movement was trying to do—regulate your nervous system so you could speak. Go ahead."

Carlos hesitated, then let his hands flap. Immediately, his anxiety decreased enough that he could organize his thoughts.

"I've been suppressing my stims since second grade," he said. "I thought I had to. But lately I've been learning that maybe I don't. It's just hard to unlearn all that shame."

Several people nodded in understanding.

"I spent years masking my stims," one person shared. "Then I realized I was spending so much energy trying to appear neurotypical that I had no energy left for actually living my life. Now I stim openly. Do some people stare? Yeah. But I'd rather be authentically autistic and functional than fake neurotypical and burned out."

After the meeting, Carlos felt lighter than he had in years. He'd spent two hours stimming freely—rocking, flapping, fidgeting—and nobody had made him feel ashamed. For the first time since childhood, he'd been in a space where his body's natural movements were acceptable.

THAT EVENING, Carlos talked to his parents.

"I went to this neurodivergent meetup today," he said at dinner.

His parents exchanged glances. They'd been supportive of his autism diagnosis, but Carlos knew they'd also been relieved when he "grew out of" the more visible autistic behaviors.

"How was it?" his mom asked carefully.

"Good. Really good, actually. Everyone was stimming openly and it was completely normal. And I realized how much energy I've been spending trying not to stim."

"What do you mean?" his dad asked.

"I mean, every day I sit perfectly still at school, even though my body wants to move. I suppress hand flapping, rocking, vocal stims—all the things that help me regulate. And it's exhausting. I've been getting tension headaches and I'm anxious all the time because I'm fighting my body's regulatory needs."

His parents looked uncomfortable.

"We thought you'd outgrown those behaviors," his mom said. "The therapists and teachers said stimming was something you needed to learn to control."

"But why?" Carlos asked. "Why do I need to control natural movements that help me function better? Because they look different? Because they make other people uncomfortable?"

"They can be distracting—" his dad started.

"To who? You or me? Because I'm more distracted when I can't stim. I'm using all my brainpower to suppress movement instead of focusing on actual tasks."

"Carlos, we're not trying to be difficult," his mom said. "We just want you to be able to function in the world. And the world can be judgmental about these things."

"I know. But I can't keep suppressing my stims just to make neurotypical people comfortable. It's hurting me. I'm looking into the research—suppressing stims leads to anxiety, burnout, and mental health problems. I'd rather stim openly and deal with some judgment than give myself a mental breakdown trying to appear normal."

His parents were quiet, processing.

"What would it look like for you to stim more?" his mom finally asked.

"Using fidget toys at school. Letting my leg bounce. Rocking when

I need to. Hand flapping when I'm excited or stressed. Humming or making sounds when it helps me focus. All the things my body naturally wants to do that I've been forcing down."

"And you think this will help?"

"I know it will. I've been experimenting a little this week, and I can already tell the difference. I'm less anxious, my headaches are better, and I can focus more easily."

His dad nodded slowly. "Okay. If this is what you need, we support you."

"But Carlos," his mom added, "if you face harassment or bullying at school because of stimming, please tell us. We'll advocate for you."

Carlos felt his eyes prick with tears. "Thanks. That means a lot."

STIMMING OPENLY at school was terrifying at first.

The first time Carlos let his hands flap in the hallway, he felt every eye on him (though realistically, most people probably didn't notice). His heart pounded. His face heated up. Every old message about being weird and needing to control himself screamed in his head.

But nothing bad happened. People walked by. Life continued. The world didn't end.

In his classes, Carlos started stimming more openly. He used his fidget cube without hiding it. He let his leg bounce visibly. He rocked slightly when thinking hard.

Some classmates asked questions: "Why do you do that with your hands?" "What's that cube thing?" "Are you okay? You're rocking."

Carlos had prepared answers: "I'm autistic and it helps me focus."

Most people just said "oh, okay" and moved on. It wasn't the big deal he'd feared.

But there were some negative reactions. One day in the cafeteria, Carlos was flapping his hands while talking excitedly to Ana about a video game, and a guy from the football team mimicked him mockingly.

"Look at me, I'm a bird," the guy said, flapping his arms exaggeratedly while his friends laughed.

Carlos felt shame crash over him—the old familiar feeling that his natural movements were wrong and mockable.

But Ana stood up. "Hey, that's not cool. He's autistic, and stimming is how he regulates. Making fun of it is literally ableist."

The guy looked embarrassed. "I didn't know—"

"Well now you do. Don't be a jerk."

After the guys left, Carlos turned to Ana. "Thanks for standing up for me."

"Of course. You shouldn't have to hide who you are because some people are ignorant."

"I was so embarrassed."

"I know. But you know what? You kept stimming after they walked away. You didn't let them make you stop."

Carlos realized she was right. His hands were still moving, still helping him regulate the emotional spike from the confrontation. In the past, he would have frozen completely, shut down, stopped stimming for days.

But he hadn't. He'd kept going.

Carlos started advocating for other autistic students' right to stim.

When a teacher told a younger student to "stop fidgeting," Carlos spoke up: "Actually, fidgeting helps lots of students focus. It's not disruptive unless it's making noise or interfering with learning."

The teacher looked surprised, but backed down.

Carlos started carrying extra fidget tools and offering them to classmates who seemed like they needed them—autistic or not. He discovered that lots of people benefited from having something to do with their hands while learning.

He also connected with other autistic students who'd been suppressing their stims. Seeing Carlos stim openly gave them permission to try it too. Soon, there was a small group of openly stimming students who supported each other.

"It's wild how just seeing someone else do it makes it feel less scary," one student told Carlos. "You're like, leading a stimming revolution."

Carlos laughed, but he kind of was. By refusing to hide his stims, he was normalizing something that autistic people had been shamed for forever.

SIX MONTHS INTO HIS "STIMMING REVOLUTION," Carlos sat in English class working on an essay. His leg bounced steadily. His fingers tapped a rhythm on his desk. His body rocked slightly as he thought.

And he was completely focused. His essay was flowing. He could think clearly. He had no headache.

His teacher walked by and paused. "Carlos, you seem really engaged with this assignment."

"I am. It's actually a really interesting topic."

"I've noticed your work has improved significantly this semester. And you seem more comfortable in class."

"I am more comfortable. I stopped suppressing my stims, and it turns out that helps me focus way better."

His teacher nodded thoughtfully. "That makes sense. Your energy's not split between self-monitoring and actual learning."

"Exactly."

After class, Carlos pulled out his phone and filmed a short video:

"Six months ago, I started openly stimming after years of suppressing it. People told me I needed to stop being 'weird' and learn to sit still. But stimming isn't weird—it's how autistic people regulate our nervous systems. And suppressing it was literally making me sick.

"So this is me saying: stim proudly. Flap your hands. Rock your body. Click your pens. Hum your songs. Do whatever helps your body feel regulated. Anyone who tells you to stop is asking you to hurt yourself for their comfort. That's not okay.

"Your stims aren't misbehavior. They're self-care. They're communication. They're beautiful.

"Don't suppress your stims. The world can adapt to you."

He posted it to TikTok, not expecting much. But within days, it had thousands of views and hundreds of comments from other autistic people:

"I needed to hear this" "I'm gonna try stimming in class tomorrow" "Thank you for normalizing this" "I've been suppressing for 20 years and I'm exhausted"

Carlos realized his personal journey of accepting his stims had become something bigger. He was part of a movement of autistic people reclaiming the right to exist in their bodies naturally, without forcing themselves into neurotypical-appearing stillness.

It was revolutionary. It was necessary. And it was beautiful.

REFLECT

1. What stims do you naturally want to do but suppress?

Think about the movements, sounds, or behaviors your body wants to engage in but you've learned to control. Hand flapping? Rocking? Bouncing? Humming? Clicking? Tapping? Be honest about what your body naturally wants to do.

____

____

____

____

____

2. Why do you suppress your stims?

Identify the messages you've received: from teachers, parents, peers, society. What have you been told about your natural movements? Why were you taught they were wrong or unacceptable?

____

____

____

____

____

3. What does it cost you to suppress your stims?

Consider the energy expenditure, the reduced focus, the anxiety, the tension headaches, the exhaustion. What are the actual consequences of fighting against your body's regulatory needs?

____

____

____

____

____

4. Have you ever been in an environment where stimming was accepted or even encouraged?

Think about spaces where you felt free to move naturally. What was different about those environments? How did you feel when you could stim freely?

____

____

____

____

____

5. What would it feel like to reclaim your stims?

Imagine moving through your day without constantly monitoring and suppressing your body's natural movements. What might change in your focus, energy, anxiety, and overall wellbeing?

____

____

____

____

____

~

Act

This week, give yourself permission to stim freely in at least one environment.

Step 1: Identify your natural stims

Make a list of movements or behaviors your body naturally wants to do:

- Hand movements (flapping, wringing, finger movements)
- Body movements (rocking, swaying, bouncing)
- Leg/foot movements (bouncing, tapping, swinging)
- Vocal stims (humming, singing, repeating words/sounds)
- Object-based stims (fidget toys, textures, clicking pens)
- Other stims (pacing, spinning, jumping)

Note which ones you currently suppress and which ones (if any) you allow.

Step 2: Understand the difference between helpful and harmful stims

Most stims are helpful—they regulate your nervous system and help you function better.

Harmful stims hurt you or others (hitting yourself, banging your head, biting until it injures, etc.). If you engage in harmful stims, work with a therapist to find alternative regulatory strategies.

But the vast majority of stims—flapping, rocking, fidgeting, humming—are helpful and should be allowed, not suppressed.

Step 3: Choose one low-stakes environment to experiment with stimming

Start small:

- At home in your room
- During homework
- While watching TV

- During video calls (where you can turn off your camera if needed)
- At the neurodivergent student meetup (if one exists)

Give yourself explicit permission: "For the next hour, I'm going to allow my body to move however it wants without suppressing anything."

Step 4: Notice what happens

When you stim freely in your chosen environment:

- Does your anxiety decrease?
- Can you focus better?
- Do you feel more comfortable in your body?
- Does your physical tension release?
- Can you think more clearly?

Document the difference between suppressed-stim time and free-stim time.

Step 5: Gradually expand to more public environments

Once you're comfortable stimming in private:

- Try stimming with close friends who are supportive
- Use fidget tools in class (less visible than hand flapping)
- Allow subtle stims in public (leg bouncing, finger movements)
- Build up to more visible stims as you feel ready

You don't have to go from fully masked to fully open overnight. Gradual desensitization to your own stim-shame is okay.

Step 6: Prepare responses to questions or comments

People might ask about your stims. Prepare simple, confident responses:

"Why are you doing that with your hands?" "It helps me focus/regulate/think. It's called stimming."

"Can you stop that? It's distracting me." "I need to do this to focus. Is

there a way we can both be comfortable?" (Maybe you can position yourself differently, or they can shift their seat)

"That's weird." "It's how my autistic brain regulates. It's normal for me."

"You're too old to do that." "Autistic people stim at all ages. There's no age limit on self-regulation."

You don't owe anyone lengthy explanations, but having a few stock phrases ready can help.

Step 7: Find stim-positive spaces

Seek out environments where stimming is normalized:

- Neurodivergent meetups or clubs
- Online autistic communities
- Autism-friendly events
- Friend groups who accept your stimming
- Disability-affirming spaces

Being around other stimming people reduces shame and increases comfort with your own stims.

Step 8: Experiment with stim tools

Try different fidget tools to find what works:

- Fidget cubes
- Stress balls
- Putty or slime
- Chewable jewelry (if you have oral stims)
- Textured objects
- Spinners
- Tangle toys
- Worry stones

Some environments may accept stim tools more readily than visible body stims, so having tools can be a bridge.

Step 9: Educate people in your life

Share information about stimming with:

- Parents: "Stimming is self-regulation, not misbehavior. Suppressing it hurts me."
- Teachers: "I focus better when I can stim. Can we find accommodations that work for both of us?"
- Friends: "This is how my autistic brain works. I'm not being weird—I'm being me."

Provide resources if they want to learn more. Many people just don't understand what stimming is or why it's necessary.

Step 10: Document your stimming journey
Keep track of:

- What stims you're allowing yourself
- How it affects your focus, anxiety, and energy
- Reactions from others
- Your own feelings about stimming openly
- Progress in reclaiming your stims

Seeing the positive changes can motivate you to continue.
Important reminders:

- Stimming is not misbehavior—it's self-regulation
- You're not "too old" to stim—autistic people stim at all ages
- Your stims aren't hurting anyone (unless they're literally harmful stims)
- Suppressing stims to make neurotypical people comfortable is not your responsibility
- Your body knows what it needs—trust those regulatory impulses
- Reclaiming your stims is an act of self-acceptance and self-care

Extension challenge:
If you feel ready, advocate for other people's right to stim:

- Speak up when you see someone shamed for stimming
- Normalize stimming by doing it openly
- Share information about stimming on social media
- Start or join a neurodivergent student group where stimming is welcomed
- Educate teachers about the importance of allowing stims in classrooms

Every time you stim openly without apologizing, you make it easier for the next neurodivergent person to do the same.

Remember: Your stims are beautiful. They're your body's way of regulating, processing, and existing in the world. Don't suppress them to satisfy people who don't understand. Stim proudly.

10

BURNOUT AND RECOVERY

Nina woke up on a Tuesday morning and couldn't get out of bed.

Not in the "I don't want to" way. In the "my body literally will not respond to my brain's commands" way.

She stared at the ceiling, trying to will herself to move. Her alarm had been going off for twenty minutes. She needed to get up, shower, get dressed, go to school. She had an AP Physics test today. She had Student Council during lunch. She had volleyball practice after school. She had SAT tutoring at 6 PM.

But her body felt like it was made of lead. Moving seemed impossible. Even thinking about moving was exhausting.

Her mom knocked on the door. "Nina! You're going to be late!"

Nina opened her mouth to respond, but no words came out. Her throat felt tight. Speaking required energy she didn't have.

The door opened. Her mom's face shifted from annoyed to concerned. "Nina? Are you okay?"

Nina wanted to say she was fine. That she'd get up in a minute. But she couldn't make her voice work. Couldn't make her body move. Couldn't do anything except lie there, feeling like every system in her body had shut down.

"I'm calling Dr. Martinez," her mom said, pulling out her phone.

Six weeks **earlier**

Nina's life looked perfect on paper.

Straight A's in all AP classes. Vice President of Student Council. Captain of the varsity volleyball team. Volunteer coordinator for the local animal shelter. Member of three clubs. Part-time job at the library. Over 200 hours of community service. Perfect attendance. Glowing teacher recommendations.

She was the kind of student college admissions officers loved. The kind of kid parents pointed to as an example. The kind of teenager who had it all figured out.

What people didn't see was the cost of maintaining that perfect image.

Nina was autistic, diagnosed at age twelve. But she'd learned to mask so thoroughly that most people forgot—or never knew in the first place. She forced herself to make eye contact even though it was uncomfortable. She participated in loud, chaotic social events even though they were sensory nightmares. She said yes to every opportunity even when she desperately needed rest. She pushed through exhaustion, sensory overload, and social overwhelm because that's what successful people did.

She'd been operating this way for years. Ignoring her body's signals that she needed to slow down. Dismissing her sensory needs as weakness. Treating her limits as obstacles to overcome rather than boundaries to respect.

"You're such a perfectionist," her friends would say admiringly.

"You make it look so easy," her teachers would comment.

"I don't know how you do it all," her parents would marvel.

Nina didn't know how she did it either. She just knew she had to. Slowing down felt like failure. Saying no felt like letting people down. Admitting she was struggling felt like proving she wasn't as capable as people thought.

So she kept pushing. Kept masking. Kept ignoring every warning sign her body and brain were giving her.

Four weeks before the crash

The first sign was sensory sensitivity increasing dramatically.

The cafeteria, which had always been overstimulating but manageable, suddenly felt unbearable. The fluorescent lights hurt Nina's eyes. The overlapping conversations felt like physical assault on her ears. The smell of food made her nauseous.

She started eating lunch in the library, where it was quieter. But even that was getting harder. The sound of pages turning, keyboards clicking, people whispering—everything was too much.

Her clothes felt wrong. Tags that she'd tolerated for years suddenly felt like knives against her skin. Certain fabrics were unbearable. Her school uniform—which she'd worn for three years—now felt like sensory torture.

"Just tough it out," she told herself. "Everyone deals with uncomfortable clothes."

Three weeks before the crash

Nina started losing abilities she'd developed through years of effort.

Eye contact, which she'd trained herself to maintain during conversations, became impossible. She physically could not make herself look at people's faces anymore.

Small talk, which she'd learned to navigate through careful observation and practice, was beyond her capability. When people asked "how are you?" she couldn't generate the automatic "good, how are you?" response. She just stood there, brain blank.

Social scripts she'd memorized—greetings, polite responses, conversation patterns—vanished from her accessible memory. She felt like she was learning to interact for the first time, except she didn't have the energy to learn.

Her teachers started commenting: "Nina, are you feeling okay? You seem distracted." "Is something going on at home? Your participation has dropped significantly." "Your last two assignments were not up to your usual standards."

Nina knew she was struggling, but she didn't know how to explain what was happening. She didn't have words for the way her brain felt like it was shutting down, system by system.

TWO WEEKS **before the crash**

The meltdowns started.

Nina had learned in childhood to suppress meltdowns in public. To hold everything together until she got home, then collapse in her room. But her capacity to suppress was disintegrating.

She had a meltdown in the school bathroom after a fire drill. The unexpected loud alarm, the chaos of evacuation, the inability to control the situation—it was too much. She ended up sobbing on the bathroom floor, unable to calm down for forty minutes.

She had a meltdown at volleyball practice when the coach made last-minute changes to the game plan. The unpredictability sent her into a panic spiral. She left practice early, something she'd never done before.

She had a meltdown at home when her mom asked a simple question about college applications. The question wasn't unreasonable, but Nina's overwhelmed brain interpreted it as one more demand in an endless list of demands. She screamed at her mom— actually screamed—then immediately felt horrible about it.

"I don't know what's wrong with me," she told her mom through tears. "I can't handle anything anymore. I'm falling apart."

"Maybe you need to cut back on some activities," her mom suggested gently.

"I can't. Colleges need to see that I'm well-rounded and committed. If I quit things now, it'll look bad on my applications."

"Nina, your mental health is more important than college applications."

"Easy for you to say. You're not the one whose entire future depends on the next eight months."

ONE WEEK before the crash

Nina stopped being able to mask entirely.

She showed up to Student Council meeting and realized she couldn't perform the "engaged, enthusiastic leader" version of herself. She sat there, mostly silent, unable to generate the energy for the social performance.

"Are you okay?" the president asked after the meeting.

"I'm fine," Nina said automatically.

But she wasn't fine. She was so far from fine that "fine" was barely visible on the horizon.

That night, Nina looked at her schedule for the next week and felt something break inside her. Every day was packed from 7 AM to 10 PM with school, activities, work, volunteering, studying. There was no space for rest. No time for recovery. No room for her to just exist without performing or producing.

She couldn't do it anymore. Her body was screaming at her to stop. Her brain was barely functioning. Every task felt insurmountable.

But she had to keep going. She just had to make it through junior year. Then she could rest. Just a few more months of pushing...

THE CRASH

Which brought her to Tuesday morning, unable to move, unable to speak, her body finally forcing the rest her brain refused to allow.

Dr. Martinez came to the house that afternoon for a home visit.

"Nina," she said gently, sitting on the edge of Nina's bed. "I think you're experiencing autistic burnout."

Nina managed to turn her head to look at the doctor.

"Autistic burnout is what happens when you push yourself beyond your limits for too long. It's not just being tired—it's a complete system shutdown. Loss of skills, extreme fatigue, inability to mask, increased sensory sensitivity, loss of speech, executive function collapse. Your body is forcing you to stop because you wouldn't stop yourself."

Tears ran down Nina's face.

"How long have you been pushing yourself without adequate rest?" Dr. Martinez asked.

Nina tried to speak. Failed. Tried again. Finally managed: "Years."

"The good news is that burnout is recoverable. The bad news is that recovery requires the one thing you're probably terrible at: actually resting."

DR. MARTINEZ EXPLAINED that autistic burnout wasn't like typical stress or exhaustion. It was a neurological shutdown that happened when autistic people exceeded their capacity for too long. Recovery required:

1. **Reducing demands** - Cutting out non-essential activities and obligations
2. **Stopping masking** - No more performing neurotypical behavior
3. **Sensory accommodation** - Creating low-stimulation environments
4. **Actual rest** - Not "productive rest," but genuine non-demanding recovery time
5. **Respecting limits** - Learning to recognize and honor capacity boundaries
6. **Time** - Burnout didn't develop overnight and wouldn't resolve overnight

"How long does recovery take?" Nina's mom asked.

"It depends on how severe the burnout is and how well someone rests during recovery. Weeks to months, usually. Sometimes longer."

"But Nina has school, and college applications, and—"

"With all respect," Dr. Martinez interrupted, "if Nina tries to maintain her current schedule, she will not recover. She'll get worse. Autistic burnout can last years if it's not properly addressed. We need to prioritize recovery now, even if it means adjusting expectations about junior year."

THE HARD DECISIONS

Over the next few days, as Nina slowly regained the ability to move and speak, she and her parents made difficult decisions:

- Medical leave from school for at least two weeks, possibly longer
- Stepping down from Student Council leadership
- Taking a break from volleyball (missing several games)
- Quitting her library job
- Dropping two of her three clubs
- Reducing volunteer hours significantly
- Rescheduling SAT tutoring for when she was recovered

Each decision felt like failure. Like she was giving up. Like she was letting everyone down.

"I'm throwing away my future," Nina cried to her mom. "Colleges are going to see that I quit everything junior year. They're going to think I'm not committed or reliable."

"Or," her mom said gently, "they're going to see a student who recognized she was burning out and made mature decisions about her health. That's actually impressive."

"No college is going to be impressed by a quitter."

"You're not quitting. You're recovering from a neurological condition. There's a difference."

WEEK I of recovery

Nina spent most of the first week in bed, in darkness, with noise-canceling headphones. Even minimal sensory input was overwhelming. Her mom brought food to her room. She had no visitors. She did nothing productive.

The guilt was crushing.

"I should be studying. I should be doing college applications. I should be catching up on homework."

But she couldn't. Her brain and body wouldn't cooperate. Reading felt impossible. Writing was beyond her. Even watching TV was too much stimulation.

She slept. She stared at the ceiling. She listened to familiar music on repeat at low volume. She ate when food appeared. She existed in the smallest possible way.

It felt like dying. But it was actually the beginning of healing.

WEEK 2-3 of recovery

Nina gradually began to tolerate more sensory input. She could spend time in other rooms of the house. She could handle short conversations. She could read for brief periods.

But she was nothing like her pre-burnout self. She couldn't mask at all. Small unexpected changes sent her into meltdowns. Executive function tasks like deciding what to eat or what to wear were impossible.

Her autistic traits were more pronounced than they'd ever been: she stimmed constantly (no energy to suppress it anymore), avoided eye contact entirely, needed everything explicitly explained, couldn't read social cues, and required extensive routine and predictability.

"Is this permanent?" she asked Dr. Martinez at a follow-up appointment. "Am I going to be like this forever?"

"No. But recovery isn't linear. Right now, your brain is in emergency conservation mode. It's redirecting all energy to essential functions. As you heal, you'll regain capacity. But Nina, you may never get back to the level of masking and pushing you were doing before. That level was unsustainable. It's what caused the burnout."

"So I'm just... less capable now?"

"No. You're learning your actual limits instead of constantly exceeding them. That's not less capable—that's sustainable."

WEEK 4-6 of recovery

Nina returned to school part-time—half days only, with accommodations:

- Reduced course load (dropped to regular classes instead of all AP)
- Extended deadlines for assignments
- Option to leave class if overwhelmed
- Lunch in a quiet room instead of cafeteria
- Permission to wear comfortable clothes instead of uniform
- No expectation to participate in extracurriculars yet

It was humbling. Nina had gone from high-achieving perfectionist to struggling student who needed extensive support.

But she was functioning. Barely, but functioning.

She noticed things she'd never noticed before:

How exhausting eye contact was (she stopped doing it) How much energy masking required (she stopped trying) How overwhelming the cafeteria was (she'd been forcing herself through sensory hell for years) How many activities she'd been doing out of obligation rather than genuine interest How little she'd been resting

"I was treating my body like a machine," she told her therapist. "Like if I just pushed hard enough, it would keep performing indefinitely. But bodies aren't machines. They need rest and accommodation and respect."

MONTH 3 of recovery

Nina was back at school full-time, but her life looked completely different:

- Modified schedule with study hall periods for rest
- Only one extracurricular (animal shelter volunteering, which she actually loved)
- No leadership positions
- Accommodations for her sensory needs and executive function challenges
- Permission to stim openly in class
- Regular breaks to prevent overwhelm

Her GPA had dropped from 4.0 to 3.6. Her resume looked less impressive. Her schedule had space in it—actual free time where she did nothing productive.

And she was okay. Not perfect. Not the high-achieving over-achiever she'd been. But okay in a sustainable, genuine way.

MONTH 6 of recovery

When college application season arrived, Nina wrote her personal essay about burnout:

*"I learned about limits the hard way: by exceeding mine until my body forced me to stop. For years, I pushed myself to maintain straight A's, lead multiple activities, and appear effortlessly capable. What people didn't see was that I'm autistic, and I was spending immense energy masking my neurodivergence while overextending myself.

I crashed. Hard. I experienced autistic burnout—a complete neurological shutdown that left me unable to function for weeks.

Recovery taught me that sustainability matters more than impressive resumes. That rest is productive, even when it looks like doing nothing. That accommodations aren't weaknesses—they're what allow me to function long-term. That my worth isn't determined by how much I can push myself beyond my limits.

I'm not the same student I was before burnout. I'm better. I'm honest about my needs. I'm realistic about my capacity. I'm building a life that works with my neurodivergence instead of fighting against it.

This isn't a story about overcoming disability. It's about learning to work with my brain instead of destroying myself trying to appear neurotypical. That's the lesson I bring to college: self-awareness, sustainability, and the courage to honor my limits."*

Her college counselor read it and cried. "Nina, this is powerful. This is real growth and self-awareness. Colleges will see that."

ONE YEAR later

Nina got into a good college—not her original dream school, but a school with strong support services for disabled students and a more reasonable pace.

Looking back, she could see the warning signs she'd ignored:

- Increasing sensory sensitivity
- Losing abilities she'd worked to develop
- More frequent meltdowns
- Complete exhaustion
- Inability to enjoy anything
- Physical symptoms (headaches, nausea, tension)
- Feeling like she was barely holding it together

"I wish I'd listened to my body earlier," she told her mom. "I could have avoided the full burnout if I'd just slowed down when the warning signs appeared."

"Maybe. But you also learned something important: your limits are real and they matter. You can't just willpower your way past them."

Nina thought about the version of herself from a year ago—the girl who thought rest was weakness and pushing past limits was strength. That girl had been heading for destruction.

This version of Nina—the one who scheduled rest, who said no to things, who stopped masking, who honored her sensory needs, who recognized burnout warning signs—was actually stronger. Because strength wasn't about pushing until you broke. It was about sustainability.

"I'm never going back to that pace," Nina said. "I know my resume looks less impressive now. I know I'm not the perfect overachiever anymore. But I'm healthy. I'm sustainable. I'm actually happy sometimes. That's worth more than any college acceptance letter."

Her mom hugged her. "I'm proud of you. Not for your accomplishments. For learning to take care of yourself."

At the neurodivergent student group Nina now attended, a newer member asked, "How do you prevent burnout?"

Nina shared what she'd learned:

"You have to respect your limits before your body forces you to. That means:

1. **Recognize warning signs:** Increased sensory sensitivity, losing abilities, more frequent meltdowns, complete exhaustion
2. **Schedule rest:** Actual recovery time, not just 'productive' relaxation
3. **Say no:** You can't do everything. Choose what matters most.
4. **Stop masking:** Or at least mask less. The energy cost is too high.
5. **Use accommodations:** They're not weaknesses—they prevent burnout
6. **Listen to your body:** When it says stop, stop. Don't wait for a crash.
7. **Build sustainability:** A B average with good mental health beats straight A's with burnout

I learned these things the hard way. You don't have to. Your body will tell you when you're approaching your limits. Listen to it.

Because burnout is brutal, and recovery is long, and prevention is so much better than trying to come back from complete shutdown."

NINA STILL HAD HARD DAYS. Days when she pushed too much and felt the warning signs of overwhelm. Days when she was tempted to go back to her old overachieving patterns.

But she'd learned to catch herself before the spiral. To rest before she crashed. To honor her limits instead of constantly exceeding them.

She was no longer the perfect, impressive, accomplishment-machine version of herself.

She was the sustainable, self-aware, actually-happy version of herself.

And that was enough.

~

REFLECT

I. **Are you currently pushing yourself beyond your limits? How do you know?**

Consider: Are you constantly exhausted? Losing abilities you used to have? Experiencing more frequent meltdowns or shutdowns? Unable to recover from normal activities? Feeling like you're barely holding it together?

____

____

____

____

____

2. **What warning signs of burnout have you been ignoring?**

Think about: Increased sensory sensitivity, difficulty with tasks that used to be manageable, loss of speech or other skills, inability to mask as effectively, more emotional dysregulation, physical symptoms, complete exhaustion that rest doesn't fix.

____

____

____

____

____

3. Why do you keep pushing past your limits?

Identify what drives you: Fear of failure? External expectations? Perfectionism? Belief that your worth is tied to productivity? Fear of disappointing others? Thinking rest is weakness?

____

____

____

____

____

4. What would it take for you to actually rest?

Consider: What stops you from resting now? What would need to change for you to prioritize recovery? What accommodations or support would help?

____

____

____

____

____

5. If you've experienced burnout before, what did recovery teach you?

Reflect on: What helped? What hindered? What would you do

differently? What boundaries do you need to maintain to prevent it happening again?

____

____

____

____

____

~

Act

This week, assess your burnout risk and take concrete steps to prevent or address it.

Step 1: Take a burnout assessment

Answer honestly:

□ I feel exhausted even after rest □ Tasks that used to be manageable now feel overwhelming □ I'm losing abilities I previously had (masking, speech, executive function, etc.) □ I'm experiencing more frequent meltdowns or shutdowns □ My sensory sensitivities have increased significantly □ I can't enjoy activities that usually bring me pleasure □ I feel like I'm barely holding it together □ Physical symptoms (headaches, nausea, tension) are constant □ I can't remember the last time I truly rested □ I'm pushing through despite clear signals to stop

Scoring:

- 0-2: Low burnout risk (but stay vigilant)
- 3-5: Moderate burnout risk (make changes now)
- 6-8: High burnout risk (immediate intervention needed)
- 9-10: Likely experiencing burnout (seek professional support and implement recovery plan)

Step 2: Identify what you can reduce or eliminate

Make three lists:

MUST DO (non-negotiable): (Example: attend school, basic hygiene, eat)

SHOULD DO (important but could be modified): (Example: homework - could request extensions; job - could reduce hours)

COULD DROP (optional, even if they look good on paper): (Example: extra clubs you don't enjoy, social obligations that drain you, activities you do for college applications but don't care about)

Look at your COULD DROP list. What can you eliminate THIS WEEK to create more recovery space?

Step 3: Schedule actual rest

Not "productive rest" like reading educational books or organizing your room. Actual, genuine, non-demanding rest:

- Lying in darkness
- Listening to familiar music
- Gentle stimming
- Being in nature (if that's regulating for you)
- Quiet time with pets
- Familiar, low-demand activities
- Sleeping

Schedule AT LEAST 2-3 hours per week of this actual rest. Put it in your calendar like any other appointment. It's not optional—it's preventive medicine.

Step 4: Identify your personal burnout warning signs

Based on past experience or current patterns, what are YOUR early warning signs?

Mine are:

WHEN YOU NOTICE THESE SIGNS, **commit to:**

- Immediately reducing demands
- Increasing rest
- Using more accommodations

- Saying no to new commitments
- Checking in with your support system

Step 5: Practice saying no
This week, say NO to at least one thing you would normally force yourself to do:

- "No, I can't take on that extra project"
- "No, I can't make it to that social event"
- "No, I need to rest instead"
- "No, I've reached my capacity"

Practice scripts:

- "I appreciate the offer, but I need to manage my energy right now."
- "I'm at capacity. I can't take on anything else."
- "That sounds great, but it's not sustainable for me right now."
- "I need to prioritize my health, so I'll have to pass."

You don't owe anyone elaborate explanations.
Step 6: Stop or reduce masking
Identify one way you're masking that's particularly exhausting:

- Forcing eye contact
- Suppressing stims
- Attending overstimulating social events
- Performing neurotypical-appearing behavior
- Ignoring sensory needs

Give yourself permission to stop doing that one thing. Your energy is finite—stop wasting it on appearing neurotypical.
Step 7: If you're currently in burnout, implement recovery protocol

Immediate actions:

- Talk to parents/guardians about medical leave or reduced schedule
- Connect with doctor/therapist about accommodations
- Eliminate all non-essential activities
- Create a sensory-friendly recovery space
- Stop all masking
- Rest aggressively (not a little rest—a LOT of rest)

Medium-term recovery:

- Work with school on accommodations (reduced course load, extended deadlines, quiet space access)
- Set boundaries with family and friends about demands
- Attend only essential activities
- Build back slowly (don't rush recovery)
- Track warning signs to prevent relapse

Long-term prevention:

- Learn to recognize limits BEFORE hitting them
- Build sustainable routines instead of pushing patterns
- Use accommodations preventively
- Schedule regular rest
- Keep life at 70-80% capacity (not 100%+)

Step 8: Document your limits
Create a personal capacity guide:
Green Zone (sustainable):

- Number of activities/classes I can handle
- Amount of socializing I can do before needing recovery
- Sensory input I can tolerate regularly
- Amount of masking I can do without harm

Yellow Zone (warning signs):

- What happens when I push past sustainable levels
- Early warning signs I need to rest
- Accommodations I need to implement

Red Zone (burnout):

- What complete overwhelm looks like for me
- Emergency protocol (who to contact, what to drop, how to recover)

Refer to this guide when making decisions about taking on new commitments.

Important reminders:

- Rest is not laziness—it's essential maintenance
- Your limits are real and deserve respect
- Burnout doesn't make you weak—pushing past limits until you break doesn't make you strong
- Accommodations prevent burnout—they're not crutches
- Your worth is not determined by productivity
- Saying no is a skill and a form of self-care
- Recovery takes time—be patient with yourself
- Preventing burnout is easier than recovering from it

If you're in crisis or severe burnout: Contact your doctor, therapist, or school counselor immediately. Burnout is a medical condition that requires intervention, not something you should try to tough out alone.

11

THE PARENT TRANSLATION GUIDE

Alex slammed her bedroom door and threw herself onto her bed, fighting back tears of frustration.

"I don't understand why you're being so difficult!" her mom's voice carried through the door. "We're just trying to help you!"

That was the problem. Alex's parents were trying to help. But their version of help felt like the opposite—more pressure, more demands, more misunderstanding of what Alex actually needed.

The fight had started over something small: Alex's mom asking her to "just quickly" run to the grocery store. But for Alex, who was autistic and already depleted from a full day of school, "quickly running to the store" meant:

- Unexpected change to her planned evening routine (major stress)
- Navigating a loud, bright, overwhelming sensory environment (the grocery store)
- Making decisions about unfamiliar products (executive function challenge)
- Interacting with cashiers (social demand when she had no energy left)

What seemed like a five-minute favor to her mom was actually an hour-long gauntlet of stress and overstimulation for Alex.

But when Alex had tried to explain this, she'd been met with: "You're being lazy. It's just a quick trip. Why do you always make everything so difficult?"

Alex wasn't trying to be difficult. She was trying to survive.

The Misunderstandings

This wasn't a one-time thing. Alex and her parents had these miscommunications constantly:

Situation 1: Eye contact

Alex's dad: "Look at me when I'm talking to you. It's disrespectful to stare at the floor."

What Alex heard: "Perform this neurotypical behavior that's uncomfortable for you, or I'll think you don't care about me."

What Alex needed her dad to understand: "Eye contact is actively painful for me. I'm listening better when I'm not forcing myself to stare at your face."

Situation 2: Transitions

Alex's mom: "We're leaving in five minutes! Why aren't you ready? I told you we had this appointment!"

What Alex heard: "You should have magically prepared for this transition despite me only mentioning it once three days ago and giving you no warning today."

What Alex needed her mom to understand: "I need more transition time than five minutes. I need explicit reminders. I need a chance to mentally prepare for changes in plans."

Situation 3: Shutdowns

Alex's parents: "Stop giving us the silent treatment. We know you're mad, but ignoring us is immature."

What Alex heard: "Your neurological shutdown is being interpreted as manipulation."

What Alex needed her parents to understand: "I'm not giving you the silent treatment. I literally cannot speak when I'm overwhelmed. It's a shutdown, not defiance."

Situation 4: Emotional responses

Alex's dad: "You're overreacting. It's not that big of a deal."

What Alex heard: "Your emotional experience is invalid and you're being dramatic."

What Alex needed her dad to understand: "My emotional intensity is part of my neurodivergence. When something feels huge to me, it IS huge to me, even if it seems small to you."

Situation 5: Executive function

Alex's mom: "How can you be smart enough for honors classes but not remember to take out the trash? You're just not trying."

What Alex heard: "Your executive function challenges aren't real. You're choosing to be irresponsible."

What Alex needed her mom to understand: "Intelligence and executive function are separate things. I can understand calculus while still struggling to remember daily tasks. It's not about effort."

AFTER THE GROCERY STORE FIGHT, Alex lay on her bed feeling hopeless. Her parents loved her—Alex knew that. But love wasn't enough if they couldn't understand Alex's actual needs.

Alex pulled out her phone and texted her therapist, Dr. Santos:

My parents don't get it. They think I'm being difficult when I'm actually just trying to survive. How do I make them understand?

Dr. Santos replied: *This is extremely common with neurodivergent teens and neurotypical parents. They literally don't understand your experience because their brains work differently. Have you considered creating a translation guide?*

A what?

A document that translates your behaviors and needs into language your parents can understand. Like a neurotypical-to-neurodivergent dictionary. We can work on it in our next session.

. . .

At her therapy appointment, Dr. Santos explained:

"Your parents see your behaviors through a neurotypical lens. When you don't make eye contact, they interpret it as disrespect because that's what it would mean for a neurotypical person. When you shut down, they think you're giving them the silent treatment because that's the only context they have for someone not responding."

"So they just assume I'm being a bad kid?"

"Not necessarily bad, but they're misinterpreting neurological differences as behavioral choices. They need education about what autism actually looks like for you specifically. A translation guide can help with that."

Dr. Santos pulled out a template:

THE PARENT TRANSLATION GUIDE *What parents see* → *What's actually happening* → *What I need*

"Let's fill this in together with your most common miscommunications," Dr. Santos suggested.

Over the next hour, Alex and Dr. Santos created the guide:

COMMUNICATION & SOCIAL

What you see: Alex doesn't make eye contact **What's actually happening:** Eye contact is physically uncomfortable and makes it harder for me to process what you're saying **What I need:** Accept that I'm listening even when I'm looking away. Judge my attention by my responses, not my eye direction.

What you see: Alex gives one-word answers **What's actually happening:** I'm either overwhelmed and can't formulate longer responses, or the question doesn't require more than a word **What I need:** If you want more detailed answers, ask more specific questions. "How was your day?" is too broad. "What was interesting in biology today?" gives me a concrete starting point.

What you see: Alex doesn't want to talk after school **What's actually happening:** I've been masking and processing sensory input all day. I'm completely drained and need time to decompress before I can engage socially, even with family. **What I need:** Let me have 30-60 minutes of quiet time when I get home before expecting conversation. I'll come find you when I'm ready to talk.

EXECUTIVE FUNCTION & MEMORY

What you see: Alex forgets things I've told her multiple times **What's actually happening:** Working memory challenges mean verbal information often doesn't stick, especially if I'm distracted or overwhelmed when you tell me **What I need:** Write things down. Text me reminders. Don't rely on verbal-only communication for important information. This isn't about not listening—my brain just doesn't retain verbal information well.

What you see: Alex can't start tasks even when she knows she needs to **What's actually happening:** Task initiation is an executive function challenge. My brain struggles to begin tasks, especially overwhelming ones, even when I want to do them **What I need:** Help me break tasks into tiny first steps. Instead of "clean your room," try "pick up three items and put them away." Sometimes I just need someone to sit with me while I start (body doubling).

What you see: Alex's room is a disaster **What's actually happening:** Organization and maintenance are executive function skills that are genuinely difficult for me. It's not laziness—my brain doesn't naturally create or maintain organizational systems **What I need:** Help me create simple systems that work with my brain. Labels, clear bins, "everything has one home" setups. And accept that my room might never be as organized as you'd like.

SENSORY & ENVIRONMENT

What you see: Alex is "being picky" about food/clothes/sounds **What's actually happening:** Sensory sensitivities make certain textures, sounds, smells, or inputs genuinely painful or overwhelming, not just mildly unpleasant **What I need:** Respect my sensory needs as real medical needs, not preferences I should "get over." Let me wear comfortable clothes, avoid painful sensory inputs, and use accommodations (headphones, sunglasses, etc.) without judgment.

What you see: Alex seems fine in public but "falls apart" at home **What's actually happening:** I mask heavily in public, suppressing my autistic traits and sensory discomfort. By the time I get home, I'm completely overwhelmed and can't mask anymore. You're seeing the accumulated stress of the day. **What I need:** Understand that home is where I decompress. If I seem more "autistic" at home than at school, that's because I finally feel safe enough to stop performing.

What you see: Alex "overreacts" to changes in plans **What's actually happening:** Unexpected changes are genuinely destabilizing for me. My brain needs predictability and advance notice to prepare for transitions. **What I need:** Give me as much advance notice as possible about plans, changes, or transitions. Even small changes need warning. "We're leaving in 5 minutes" doesn't work—I need at least 30-60 minutes notice.

EMOTIONAL REGULATION

What you see: Alex seems to overreact to criticism **What's actually happening:** Rejection Sensitive Dysphoria (part of my neurodivergence) makes criticism feel intensely painful, way out of proportion to the actual feedback **What I need:** Lead with positive feedback before constructive criticism. Be very explicit that criticism of my behavior isn't rejection of me as a person. Understand that my emotional pain is real, even if the trigger seems small to you.

What you see: Alex shuts down and won't talk **What's actually happening:** This is a neurological shutdown, not the silent treatment. When I'm overwhelmed, I lose the ability to speak. It's not voluntary or manipulative. **What I need:** Give me space during shutdowns. Don't demand that I talk. Let me recover in quiet, low-stimulation environments. I'll communicate when I'm able—often through text first.

What you see: Alex gets really intense about certain topics **What's actually happening:** Special interests are a core part of autism. When I care about something, I care deeply and want to share that enthusiasm. **What I need:** Let me info-dump about my interests sometimes. You don't have to be equally interested, but showing that you value my passion means a lot. If you're not up for a long discussion, just say "I don't have energy for a deep dive right now, but I love that you're passionate about this."

WHAT HELPS

Things that make life easier for me:

- Advance notice about plans (the more notice, the better)
- Written information instead of just verbal
- Clear, specific instructions ("put your shoes in the closet" not "clean up")
- Predictable routines
- Quiet, low-stimulation home environment
- Permission to use accommodations (headphones, fidgets, etc.) without comment
- Time to decompress after school/social events
- Respect for my "no" when I'm at capacity
- Seeing my behaviors as symptoms/needs rather than defiance
- Patience when I'm struggling

Things that make life harder:

- Last-minute changes to plans
- Being pushed past my limits "for my own good"
- "Just try harder" or "just get over it"
- Forcing eye contact or other neurotypical performances
- Loud, chaotic family environments
- Being compared to neurotypical peers
- Having my shutdowns or meltdowns treated as manipulation
- Being told my sensory needs are "picky" or "dramatic"

ALEX PRINTED out the guide and left it on the kitchen table with a note:

Mom and Dad,

I know we keep having misunderstandings. I know you think I'm being difficult or not trying. But there's a gap between how you see my behavior and what's actually happening for me.

I made this guide with my therapist to help you understand my autism better. I'm not asking you to fix me or make me more neurotypical. I'm asking you to understand how my brain works and what I actually need.

I love you. I know you love me. But love without understanding is making both of us frustrated.

- Alex

THAT EVENING, Alex heard her parents reading the guide in the living room. She caught snippets of conversation:

"I had no idea eye contact was actually painful..." "I thought shutdowns were just teenage attitude..." "This explains so much about the grocery store fight..."

Eventually, both parents came to Alex's room and knocked.

"Can we talk?" her mom asked.

Alex braced herself for defensiveness or dismissal. Instead, her dad said:

"We read your guide. We... had no idea about a lot of this stuff."

"We thought we understood autism because we read some books when you were diagnosed," her mom added. "But those books were mostly about little kids. We didn't know how it showed up for teenagers, or how much energy you were spending masking, or how painful some things were for you."

"So... you believe me?" Alex asked cautiously.

"Yes," her dad said firmly. "And we're sorry. We've been misinterpreting your needs as behavior problems. That's on us, not you."

Her mom sat on the edge of Alex's bed. "Can you help us understand what changed? You seemed fine as a kid, and now..."

"I wasn't fine," Alex interrupted gently. "I was masking really hard. Little kids can get away with more autistic behaviors because everyone expects kids to be weird sometimes. But the older I got, the more pressure there was to be 'normal.' So I pushed myself to seem more neurotypical, and it worked so well that you forgot I was autistic. But all that masking has been exhausting me."

"The guide said you can't mask as much at home because you're drained," her dad said. "Is that why you seem... more autistic lately?"

"Yes. Home is the only place I feel safe enough to unmask. But that means you see me at my most depleted, most overstimulated, least capable of performing neurotypical behavior."

"So when we ask you to do something and you can't, it's not that you won't—it's that you genuinely don't have the capacity at that moment?"

"Exactly."

Her parents looked at each other, having one of those silent married-couple conversations.

"We need to change how we're approaching this," her mom said. "We've been treating your autism like something you need to overcome instead of something we need to accommodate."

"Can you help us learn?" her dad asked. "Tell us when we're misunderstanding? We can't promise we'll get it right all the time, but we want to try."

Alex felt tears prick her eyes. "Really?"

"Really. You're our kid. We love you. And we want to love you in ways that actually help instead of making things harder."

Over the next few weeks, things gradually improved:

The grocery store situation (revised):

Before: "Alex, can you quickly run to the store?" After: "Alex, I need to go grocery shopping tomorrow. Want to come with me at 3 PM, or would you rather I go alone? If you come, we can take headphones and I'll handle the checkout interaction."

Alex's response: "I'll come. Thanks for the advance notice and accommodations."

The eye contact situation (revised):

Before: "Look at me when I'm talking to you!" After: Dad learned to gauge Alex's attention by her responses and body language, not eye direction.

Result: Conversations became less stressful for Alex, and ironically, Alex sometimes made eye contact naturally when she wasn't being forced to.

The shutdown situation (revised):

Before: "Stop ignoring us!" After: When Alex shut down, her parents recognized it and texted: "We see you're shutdown. Take the time you need. Let us know when you can communicate again."

Result: Shutdowns resolved faster because Alex wasn't also dealing with guilt and pressure to perform.

The transition situation (revised):

Before: "We're leaving in 5 minutes!" After: "Alex, we have that dentist appointment tomorrow at 3 PM. I'll remind you tomorrow morning, then give you a 60-minute warning, 30-minute warning, and 10-minute warning."

Result: Transitions became manageable instead of crisis-inducing.

The executive function situation (revised):

Before: "Just clean your room!" After: "Let's break this down. First step: pick up dirty clothes and put them in the hamper. Come get me when that's done and we'll do the next step."

Result: Tasks actually got completed because they were broken down into manageable pieces.

IT WASN'T PERFECT. Alex's parents still made mistakes. They'd forget and demand things without advance notice, or misinterpret behaviors, or get frustrated when Alex couldn't do something that seemed simple.

But now, Alex could say: "Hey, remember the translation guide? This is one of those situations where what you're seeing isn't what's actually happening."

And her parents would pause, reconsider, and adjust their approach.

One evening, Alex overheard her mom talking to her aunt on the phone:

"I used to think Alex was being difficult. But it turns out she was working twice as hard as other kids just to seem normal. Now that I understand what she actually needs, our relationship is so much better. I just wish I'd understood sooner."

Alex felt something warm bloom in her chest. Understanding. That's all she'd wanted.

ALEX STARTED SHARING her translation guide template with other neurodivergent teens in her online support group. Other teens adapted it for their own needs:

"I made one for ADHD! It's helping my parents understand why I interrupt and forget things."

"I did one for sensory processing disorder! My mom finally gets why certain foods make me gag."

"My parents laminated mine and put it on the fridge so they can reference it!"

The guide had become a tool not just for Alex, but for lots of neurodivergent teens trying to bridge the understanding gap with their neurotypical parents.

Dr. Santos was proud. "You created something that's helping people. That's powerful."

"I just wanted my parents to get it," Alex said. "Turns out a lot of kids needed their parents to get it too."

SIX MONTHS LATER, Alex's relationship with her parents had transformed.

Were there still misunderstandings? Yes. Did her parents still sometimes default to neurotypical assumptions? Yes. But the fundamental dynamic had shifted.

Instead of:

- Parent sees behavior → assumes defiance → punishes/criticizes
- Alex feels misunderstood → shuts down → relationship deteriorates

Now:

- Parent sees behavior → checks translation guide → asks clarifying questions
- Alex explains need → parent adjusts approach → relationship strengthens

At a family dinner, Alex's younger sister (also autistic but not yet diagnosed) was having a meltdown about food texture.

"Just eat it," Alex's aunt said. "You're being ridiculous."

Alex's dad intervened immediately: "She's not being ridiculous. She has sensory sensitivities. Let's find something else she can eat."

After dinner, Alex hugged her dad. "Thanks for sticking up for her."

"I learned from you," her dad said. "I used to think kids were just being picky. Now I know better. I'm going to talk to your mom about getting your sister evaluated too."

FOR ALEX'S BIRTHDAY, her parents gave her a framed copy of a quote they'd written:

"Love is learning the language of the person you love. Thank you for teaching us your language. We're still learning, but we're trying. We love you—for exactly who you are."

Alex hung it on her bedroom wall.

She still had hard days. Days when her parents forgot to accommodate her needs, or when the neurotypical world felt impossible to navigate. But home had become safer. Her family had become a place where she could be authentically autistic without constant misunderstanding.

The translation guide hadn't fixed everything. But it had opened a door to mutual understanding. And that made all the difference.

~

REFLECT

1. What do your parents/family misunderstand about your neurodivergence?

Think about the times when your family interprets your needs as defiance, laziness, or attitude. What behaviors do they see one way when the reality is completely different?

____

____

____

____

____

2. Have you tried to explain your needs to your family? What happened?

Consider: Did they listen? Dismiss you? Get defensive? Not understand? Did you have the language to explain, or were you struggling to articulate what you needed?

____

____

____

____

____

3. What would change in your family relationships if your parents truly understood your experience?

Imagine: How would interactions be different if they knew why you do what you do? How would you feel if your needs were recognized and accommodated?

____

____

____

____

____

4. What stops you from creating your own translation guide?

Identify barriers: Fear they won't listen? Don't know how to explain? Too exhausted to try? Worried about making things worse? Feeling like you shouldn't have to explain?

____

____

____

____

____

5. Are there family members who DO understand? What's different about those relationships?

Think about: Who gets it? Why? What do they do differently? Can those relationships model what's possible?

____

____

____

____

____

❧

ACT

This week, create your own parent translation guide and share it with your family.

Step 1: Identify your most common miscommunications

List 5-10 situations where your parents/family regularly misunderstand your behavior:

Examples:

- They think you're being disrespectful when you don't make eye contact
- They think you're lazy when executive function makes tasks hard
- They think you're giving them attitude when you're actually shutdown
- They think you're overreacting when RSD makes criticism painful
- They think you're being picky when sensory issues make things unbearable

Step 2: Use the translation guide format

For each miscommunication, fill in:

What you see: [How parents interpret the behavior] **What's actually happening:** [The neurological/sensory/executive function reality] **What I need:** [Specific accommodations or changes in approach]

Be honest but not aggressive. The goal is education, not blame.

Step 3: Add "What Helps" and "What Makes Things Harder" sections

What helps:

- Specific accommodations that work for you
- Communication styles that you respond to
- Environmental modifications that reduce stress
- Ways they can support you

What makes things harder:

- Demands that overwhelm you
- Phrases that trigger RSD or shutdown
- Situations that exceed your capacity

- Comparisons or expectations that don't fit your neurodivergence

Step 4: Personalize it
Add sections relevant to YOUR specific neurodivergence:

- ADHD: Time blindness, executive function, hyperfocus, RSD
- Autism: Sensory needs, masking, special interests, social communication, shutdowns/meltdowns
- Dyslexia: Reading challenges, processing time, accommodations
- Multiple diagnoses: How they interact and compound

Step 5: Include resources
At the end, add:

- Links to articles/videos by neurodivergent people
- Books written by autistic/ADHD adults (not just about them)
- Recommendations for parent support groups
- Your therapist's contact info if they're willing to meet with your parents

Help them understand this isn't just your opinion—it's documented neurodivergent experience.

Step 6: Choose your delivery method
Options:

- **Print it and leave it with a note** (like Alex did)
- **Email it with explanation** (gives them time to process before discussing)
- **Present it during family meeting** (if your family does structured discussions)

- **Have therapist present it** (if parents are more receptive to professionals)
- **Share it in family therapy** (neutral space with mediator)

Choose the method most likely to be received well by YOUR family.

Step 7: Prepare for possible responses

Best case: They read it, have realizations, apologize for misunderstandings, ask how to do better

Likely case: They're surprised, somewhat defensive, need time to process, gradually make changes

Difficult case: They dismiss it, say you're making excuses, refuse to accommodate

For difficult responses, have a plan:

- Therapist can advocate for you
- School counselor can educate them
- Connect them with other parents of neurodivergent kids
- Set boundaries: "If you won't accommodate my needs, I'll spend more time in my room/with friends/etc."

Step 8: Follow up with communication

After they've had time to read it:

If they're receptive:

- Answer their questions
- Give specific examples when they need clarification
- Acknowledge when they make efforts to accommodate
- Update the guide as you learn more about your needs

If they're resistant:

- Don't abandon the guide—revisit it periodically
- Point back to it when miscommunications happen:

"Remember the translation guide? This is one of those situations"

- Seek support elsewhere if family can't provide it
- Know that their resistance isn't about you being wrong—it's about them needing to change

Step 9: Create a quick-reference version
Make a simplified one-page version they can reference easily:
QUICK GUIDE: How to Support Me
Communication:

- I need written reminders for important info
- Give me 1-hour advance notice for transitions
- When I'm quiet, I might be shutdown (not attitude)

Environment:

- I need quiet decompress time after school
- I need control over sensory input (lights, sounds)
- My room might be messy—that's okay

Emotional:

- I'm sensitive to criticism (RSD is real)
- I'm not overreacting—emotions are intense for me
- I need explicit reassurance, not hints

Tasks:

- Break big tasks into tiny steps
- I struggle with task initiation (not laziness)
- Executive function challenges are real

Put this on the fridge or somewhere visible so parents can reference it easily.

Step 10: Document changes
Track when your parents make efforts to understand and
accommodate:
Positive changes I've noticed:

- Dad stopped demanding eye contact
- Mom gives me advance notice about plans
- They ask "what do you need?" instead of assuming
- They reference the guide when confused

Acknowledging progress encourages more progress.
Important reminders:

- You shouldn't HAVE to explain your neurodivergence, but
  doing so can improve your family life
- Your parents' initial response (defensiveness, dismissal)
  isn't necessarily permanent
- Some parents need time to process and unlearn
  assumptions
- Education is ongoing—one guide won't fix everything
- If your parents refuse to understand, that's about them,
  not you
- You deserve to be understood and accommodated
- Other neurodivergent people's families CAN be your
  support system if your own family isn't

If your parents aren't receptive:
You still benefit from having articulated your needs clearly.
You can:

- Use the guide for yourself (self-validation)
- Share it with supportive adults (teachers, counselors,
  relatives)
- Save it for college (roommates, partners, friends)

- Connect with other neurodivergent people whose families DO get it
- Know that your needs are legitimate even if your family doesn't validate them

Your family's understanding is not required for your needs to be real.

12

———————

FINDING YOUR TRIBE

Liam sat alone at lunch, as usual, scrolling through his phone while half-eating a sandwich. Around him, the cafeteria buzzed with conversation and laughter—social groups that had formed naturally over years of shared experiences and mutual understanding.

Liam had never quite figured out how to be part of those groups.

It wasn't that he didn't have friends. He had a few people he talked to in classes, people who were nice to him, people who'd include him in group projects. But he didn't have *his people*. He didn't have a group that felt like home.

At seventeen, Liam had spent his entire life feeling like an outsider looking in. Like everyone else had been given an instruction manual for being human that he'd somehow missed. He was autistic —diagnosed at age nine—but knowing why he was different didn't make the loneliness any easier.

He watched a group of guys at the next table laughing at some inside joke, the kind of effortless camaraderie that Liam had tried and failed to replicate countless times. He'd join conversations but say the wrong thing. He'd try to be funny but miss the timing. He'd share something he was excited about and watch people's eyes glaze over.

"Maybe I'm just meant to be alone," Liam thought, not for the first time.

THE DISCOVERY

That night, Liam was scrolling through TikTok when a video appeared on his feed: "Things autistic people do that we thought were universal but apparently aren't."

Curious, he clicked.

The creator listed behaviors: "Practicing conversations before they happen. Repeating phrases from movies. Getting unreasonably attached to specific objects. Needing detailed information about plans before agreeing to them. Having to mentally prepare for phone calls like they're Olympic events."

Liam sat up straighter. He did ALL of those things. He'd thought everyone did.

He scrolled through the comments and found thousands of autistic people saying "YES, THIS" and "I thought I was the only one!" and "Finally someone gets it!"

Liam spent the next three hours falling down a rabbit hole of neurodivergent content creators. Autistic adults talking about their experiences. ADHD teens explaining executive dysfunction. People discussing masking, stimming, special interests, sensory issues—all the things Liam had been experiencing his whole life but had never heard other people articulate.

For the first time in seventeen years, Liam didn't feel alone.

THE ONLINE COMMUNITY

The next day, Liam created an account on a neurodivergent Discord server he'd found linked in one of the TikTok videos.

He lurked for a few days, reading conversations, getting a feel for the community. People were discussing everything from meltdown management to special interests to the exhaustion of masking. They used terms Liam had never heard but immediately understood. They shared experiences that mirrored his own with startling accuracy.

Finally, he introduced himself in the new-members channel:

Hi, I'm Liam. I'm 17 and autistic. I've always felt really alone and like nobody understands me. I found this server through TikTok and everyone here seems to actually get what it's like. So... hi.

The responses came quickly:

Welcome! You're definitely not alone here.

Hi Liam! What are your special interests?

Fellow 17yo autistic here - this community has been life-changing for me. Glad you found us!

Welcome to the tribe! 🤍

Liam felt something warm bloom in his chest. These people didn't know him, but they already understood him better than people he'd known for years.

Over the next few weeks, Liam became active in the server. He participated in discussions, shared memes, vented about struggles, celebrated wins. For the first time in his life, he could be completely himself without explanation or apology.

When he mentioned stimming with a specific fidget toy, people asked where he got it instead of why he needed it.

When he info-dumped about his special interest in linguistics, people engaged enthusiastically instead of looking bored.

When he said he was having a shutdown and couldn't respond, people just said "take care of yourself" instead of demanding explanations.

The relief was overwhelming. This was what connection was supposed to feel like.

THE DIFFERENCE

The contrast between his online neurodivergent friends and his in-person neurotypical acquaintances became starkly clear.

With neurotypical people at school:

Liam: "I can't go to that party, it'll be too overwhelming." Them: "Just try it! You might have fun!" *[Liam has to explain sensory overload, social exhaustion, the difference between being anxious and being autistic]*

With neurodivergent people online:

Liam: "I can't go to that party, it'll be too overwhelming." Them: "Totally get it. Parties are sensory hell. Want to have a quiet hangout instead?" *[No explanation needed]*

WITH NEUROTYPICAL PEOPLE:

Liam: *accidentally interrupts someone* Them: "Rude. Let me finish." *[Liam feels shame, doesn't understand what social rule he violated]*

With neurodivergent people:

Liam: *accidentally interrupts someone* Them: "Oh sorry, we both talked at once. You go first." *[No judgment, just practical acknowledgment]*

WITH NEUROTYPICAL PEOPLE:

Liam: "I'm really interested in historical linguistics and language evolution and—" Them: *eyes glazing over* "That's... nice." *[Liam learns to suppress his enthusiasm]*

With neurodivergent people:

Liam: "I'm really interested in historical linguistics and—" Them: "Oh that's cool! Have you looked into Proto-Indo-European? I went down a rabbit hole about that last month." *[Genuine interest, mutual enthusiasm]*

The neurodivergent community didn't just tolerate Liam's autistic traits—they understood them, related to them, and often shared them.

THE IN-PERSON MEETUP

Two months after joining the Discord, someone posted about an in-person neurodivergent teen meetup happening in a nearby city.

Liam's immediate reaction was anxiety—meeting new people was always stressful, even neurodivergent people.

But his online friends encouraged him:

You should go! In-person ND spaces are amazing.

I was nervous about my first meetup too, but it was so worth it. Everyone gets it.

Just FYI - the meetup is sensory-friendly. Quiet room, dim lights, stim toys available, no pressure to socialize if you're overwhelmed.

That last part convinced Liam. He asked his mom to drive him.

"You're going to meet people from the internet?" his mom asked nervously.

"It's a supervised meetup for neurodivergent teens. There are adult facilitators. It's at the community center."

"And you actually want to go? You usually avoid social events."

"This is different. These are my people."

Liam walked into the community center meeting room and immediately noticed the difference from typical teen social spaces.

It was quiet—not silent, but without the overwhelming chaos of a school cafeteria or party. The lights were dimmed. Tables along the walls held fidget toys, coloring supplies, puzzles, and other stim-friendly items. Some teens were talking in small groups. Others were sitting alone, stimming with toys or drawing. Nobody was forcing interaction.

A facilitator greeted him. "Hi! First time here?"

"Yeah. I'm Liam."

"Welcome! No pressure to socialize if you don't want to. We have a structured activity in about twenty minutes, but until then, just hang out however you're comfortable. There's a quiet room next door if you need a break."

Liam found a seat and pulled out a fidget cube, looking around. Everyone here was openly stimming—rocking, flapping hands, clicking pens, fiddling with toys. Nobody was hiding it. Nobody was apologizing for it.

A girl about his age sat down nearby. "Hey, I'm Maya. Is this your first time?"

"Yeah. I'm Liam."

"Cool. What brings you here?"

"I found a neurodivergent Discord and people mentioned these meetups. I've never really had... people who get it, I guess."

"I felt the same way before I found this group. Now I come every month. It's the only place where I don't have to mask at all."

As they talked, Liam noticed something remarkable: the conversation flowed naturally. There were none of the awkward pauses where he didn't know what to say, none of the moments where he misunderstood what was expected, none of the exhaustion of trying to decode hidden meanings.

Maya was direct. She asked clear questions. She info-dumped about her special interest (astronomy) and was genuinely interested when Liam shared his (linguistics). When they both started talking at the same time, they laughed and easily worked out who would go first. When Liam needed a moment to process something, Maya just waited without filling the silence with awkward small talk.

This was what conversation was supposed to feel like.

THE STRUCTURED ACTIVITY was a discussion about dealing with sensory overload at school. The facilitator, Alex (who was also autistic), led the conversation but didn't force anyone to participate.

Teens shared their experiences:

"The cafeteria is unbearable. I eat lunch in the library every day."

"Fire drills are the worst. No warning, just sudden loud noise and chaos."

"I hate fluorescent lights. They give me headaches and make it hard to focus."

Liam found himself sharing: "I wear noise-canceling headphones between classes, but teachers make me take them off during class even though I focus better with them."

Several people nodded in understanding. No one asked "why do you need headphones?" or "can't you just deal with the noise?" They just got it.

Someone shared a strategy that had worked for them. Another person offered a different perspective. The conversation was practical, supportive, and completely free of judgment.

For the first time in his life, Liam was in a room full of people who didn't think he was weird or too sensitive or making a big deal out of nothing. They shared his struggles. They validated his experiences. They offered solutions from their own trial and error.

AFTER THE FORMAL DISCUSSION, people broke into smaller groups. Liam ended up talking with Maya and two others—Jordan (ADHD) and Sam (autistic and dyslexic).

They talked about everything: school struggles, special interests, favorite stimming methods, the exhaustion of masking, family members who didn't understand, the neurodivergent content creators they followed.

At one point, Jordan interrupted himself mid-sentence and said, "Sorry, I just had three different thoughts at once and lost the original point."

Everyone laughed in recognition.

"That's such an ADHD mood," Sam said.

"My brain does that too," Maya added. "Though for me it's more like I start talking about one thing and then my brain connects it to seventeen other things and suddenly I'm on a completely different topic."

"Info-dumping web style," Liam said. "I do that all the time."

"See, this is why I love hanging out with neurodivergent people," Jordan said. "Nobody's like 'stay on topic' or 'you're being random.' We just... follow the thought patterns."

Liam realized Jordan was right. In this conversation, nobody was monitoring themselves constantly, making sure they weren't being "too much" or "too weird." They were just... being themselves. And everyone understood.

. . .

AS THE MEETUP ENDED, Maya gave Liam her Discord username. "You should join our group chat. We hang out online between meetups."

"Yeah, definitely," Liam said.

Walking to the car, Liam's mom asked, "How was it?"

"It was..." Liam struggled to find words for the feeling. "It was like I'd been holding my breath my whole life and finally got to breathe."

His mom's eyes got teary. "I'm so glad you found your people."

"Me too."

THE TRANSFORMATION

Over the next few months, Liam's life changed in ways both subtle and profound.

At school:

Liam still didn't have a big friend group in the traditional sense. But he no longer felt desperately lonely during lunch. He had people who understood him—even if they weren't physically present. He could text his Discord friends when something hard happened and get immediate understanding and support.

He also started noticing other students who seemed similarly isolated. One day, he saw a younger student eating alone, stimming with a fidget spinner.

"Hey," Liam said, sitting down nearby. "Cool fidget spinner."

The kid looked up, surprised and wary.

"I'm Liam. I'm autistic. I use fidget cubes."

The kid's expression shifted from wary to cautiously hopeful. "I'm Max. I'm autistic too."

"There's a neurodivergent teen meetup at the community center once a month. And a Discord server. Want the info?"

Max's face lit up. "Really? Yes!"

Liam shared the information, remembering how isolated he'd felt just months ago. If he could help one person find community earlier than he had, that mattered.

. . .

AT HOME:

Liam's relationship with his parents improved. He'd always felt like they tried to understand but couldn't quite get there. But after finding his community, Liam had language for his experiences that he hadn't had before.

"You know how you're always asking why I get so upset about changes in plans?" Liam said to his mom one day. "I learned that autistic people often have a thing called 'monotropic thinking'—we focus deeply on what we're expecting to happen, and disruptions to that are genuinely destabilizing, not just mildly annoying like they might be for neurotypical people."

"That makes so much sense," his mom said. "I've been treating it like you're being inflexible when it's actually about how your brain processes expectations and change."

"Exactly. And my neurodivergent friends do the same thing, so I know it's not just me being difficult."

Having community didn't just help Liam—it helped his family understand him better.

ONLINE:

The Discord server became Liam's home base. He logged on daily, participating in voice chats, sharing memes, offering support to newer members, and receiving support when he needed it.

When he had a meltdown at school, he came home and vented in the server. People understood immediately—they'd all been there. They offered strategies. They validated his feelings. They reminded him that meltdowns didn't make him broken.

When he discovered a new special interest (constructed languages), he found people in the server who shared that interest and spent hours discussing it with them.

When he needed to info-dump about something, he could post a long rambling message and people would actually read it and engage with it.

The server had channels for everything: venting, celebrating wins, sharing special interests, discussing accommodations, memes, voice chatting, even a quiet channel for people who were overwhelmed and just needed low-demand presence.

It was a space designed by and for neurodivergent people. And it felt like home in a way that physical spaces rarely did.

THE MEETUP COMMUNITY:

Liam became a regular at the monthly meetups. He got to know the other attendees. Inside jokes developed. Friendships formed.

They organized additional hangouts outside the official meetups —quiet movie viewings where everyone could bring stim toys and wear headphones if needed, park meetups where people could walk and talk (parallel play for humans, someone called it), and online game sessions where they could hang out together without the demands of in-person socializing.

One month, the meetup theme was "celebrating our neurodivergence." People shared what they loved about being neurodivergent:

"I love how deeply I experience things. When I love something, I LOVE it with my whole self."

"I love my special interests. They bring me so much joy."

"I love that I see patterns and connections other people miss."

"I love my autistic friends. They're the most genuine, loyal, accepting people I've ever met."

When it was Liam's turn, he said: "I love that I found all of you. For the first time in my life, I don't feel alone. I feel understood. I feel like I belong."

SIX MONTHS LATER:

Liam sat at his usual lunch table at school, scrolling through his phone. To an outside observer, nothing had changed. He was still physically alone.

But Liam wasn't lonely anymore.

He had a Discord notification—Maya sending him a meme about autistic communication styles that made him laugh out loud.

He had a text from Jordan asking if he wanted to join their Minecraft server later.

He had plans to go to the meetup that weekend, where he'd see Sam and the others.

He had a community of people who understood him without explanation. Who celebrated his neurodivergence instead of just tolerating it. Who made him feel like being autistic wasn't a barrier to connection—it was sometimes the very thing that created connection.

His mom had asked him recently if he was happier.

"Yeah," Liam had said. "I found my tribe."

"Your tribe?"

"The neurodivergent community. People who get it. People like me."

His mom had smiled. "You've been smiling more. Talking more. You seem lighter."

"That's what happens when you stop spending all your energy trying to translate yourself to people who don't speak your language. When you find people who already understand you."

AT THE NEXT MEETUP, a new person attended—a girl named Sophie who looked terrified and overwhelmed.

Liam remembered that feeling. He walked over.

"Hey, I'm Liam. First time here?"

"Yeah," Sophie said quietly. "I've never been around other autistic people before. Just... neurotypical people who don't really get it."

"I was the same way six months ago," Liam said. "It's different here. You don't have to explain everything or apologize for being yourself. People just understand."

"Really?"

"Really. Welcome to the tribe."

Sophie's expression shifted from anxious to cautiously hopeful—the same shift Liam had felt when Maya had welcomed him months ago.

This was what community did. It took isolated people and showed them they weren't alone. It took people who'd spent their lives feeling broken and showed them they were just different. It took people who'd never felt understood and gave them a space where understanding was the default.

Liam had spent seventeen years feeling like an alien on the wrong planet.

Now he knew: he wasn't an alien. He was just on a planet designed for a different neurotype. But he'd found his people—the other "aliens," the neurodivergent community who'd been here all along, creating spaces where difference was celebrated rather than pathologized.

He wasn't alone. He'd never have to be alone again.

REFLECT

1. Do you feel understood by the people around you?

Think honestly: Do you have people who truly get you without constant explanation? Or are you always translating yourself, justifying your needs, explaining your experiences?

____

____

____

____

____

2. Have you ever experienced the relief of being around other neurodivergent people?

If yes: What was different about those interactions? If no: What stops you from seeking out neurodivergent community?

____

____

____

____

____

3. What would it feel like to be in a space where your neurodivergence was the norm, not the exception?

Imagine: A place where stimming is normal, where sensory needs are accommodated by default, where communication styles match yours, where you don't have to mask or explain.

____

____

____

____

____

4. Are you isolated? If so, is it by choice or circumstance?

Consider: Do you avoid social situations because they're exhausting with neurotypical people? Would you engage more if you had neurodivergent community? Or do you genuinely prefer solitude?

____

____

____

____

____

5. What's stopping you from seeking out your tribe?

Identify barriers: Not knowing where to find community? Social anxiety? Fear of not being "autistic/ADHD/neurodivergent enough"? Transportation? Parents' resistance? Time? Energy?

____

____

____

____

____

$\sim$

ACT

This week, take one concrete step toward finding your neurodivergent community.

Step 1: Identify what type of community you're seeking

Different options for different needs:

Online community (good for: immediate access, low energy, trying things out, connecting across distance)

- Discord servers for neurodivergent teens
- Reddit communities (r/autism, r/ADHD, r/neurodiversity)
- TikTok/Instagram neurodivergent creators and their communities
- Facebook groups for neurodivergent teens
- Online forums specific to your diagnosis

In-person community (good for: deeper connections, face-to-face interaction, local support, embodied presence)

- Neurodivergent teen meetups (check community centers, libraries, disability organizations)
- Support groups through therapists or clinics
- School clubs for neurodivergent students
- Special interest groups where neurodivergent people tend to congregate (certain hobby groups, gaming communities, etc.)

Hybrid (best of both worlds)

- Online community that also organizes in-person meetups
- School group that has online chat between meetings
- Local group with digital resources

Step 2: Find specific communities
To find online communities:

- Search "[your diagnosis] teen Discord server"
- Look in the descriptions/bios of neurodivergent content creators you follow
- Ask in comments on TikTok/Instagram: "Does anyone know good neurodivergent teen communities?"
- Check r/neurodiversity for community recommendations

To find in-person communities:

- Google "[your city] neurodivergent teen meetup"
- Call local disability organizations and ask about teen groups
- Ask your therapist if they know of any groups
- Check library and community center event calendars
- Ask your school counselor about starting a neurodivergent student club if none exists

Step 3: Join or attend (take the leap)
For online communities:

- Create an account/join the server
- Lurk for a few days to get the vibe
- Read the rules and intro channels
- Introduce yourself when ready (even just "Hi, I'm [name], I'm [diagnosis], happy to be here")

- Start small—react to messages, answer questions, gradually participate more

For in-person meetups:

- RSVP or just show up (check if registration is needed)
- Tell a parent/trusted adult where you're going
- Bring a stim toy or comfort item
- Know that you can leave if it's overwhelming
- Understand that first times are always awkward—give it at least 2-3 tries before deciding

Step 4: Engage authentically
When you join community:
DO:

- Be yourself (unmask as much as feels safe)
- Share your experiences honestly
- Ask questions
- Offer support to others
- Respect boundaries and community guidelines
- Give it time—community building takes multiple interactions

DON'T:

- Fake interest or mask heavily (defeats the purpose)
- Compare your neurodivergence to others ("I'm not as autistic as...")
- Trauma dump immediately (build trust first)
- Expect instant best friends (relationships develop over time)
- Give up after one interaction

Step 5: Identify your people within the community

Not everyone in a neurodivergent space will be YOUR people. That's okay. Look for:

- People with similar interests or special interests
- Communication styles that match yours
- People who energize rather than drain you
- Those who reciprocate engagement
- People you genuinely enjoy, not just people who tolerate you

Communities have variety—find your subset within the larger group.

Step 6: Contribute to community

Once you're comfortable:

- Share resources that helped you
- Welcome new members (pay it forward like Liam did)
- Start conversations about topics that interest you
- Organize activities (game nights, special interest discussions, etc.)
- Be the friend you wish you'd had

Community isn't just about what you get—it's about what you give.

Step 7: Balance online and offline life

Signs you've found good community:

- You feel energized after interactions (even if tired)
- You can be yourself without constant explanation
- You feel understood and validated
- You're learning and growing
- You have people to share joy and struggles with
- You feel less alone

Signs you need to adjust:

- Community is draining you
- Drama is constant
- People are toxic or invalidating
- You're spending so much time online you're isolated IRL
- The community is reinforcing negative patterns

Good community should improve your life, not become your entire life.

Step 8: If you can't find community, create it

If there are no neurodivergent communities in your area:

Start a school club:

- Talk to your counselor about starting a neurodivergent/neurodiversity club
- Recruit even just 2-3 people to start
- Create a space for neurodivergent students to connect

Create an online space:

- Start a Discord server
- Create a group chat
- Build the community you wish existed

Connect one-on-one:

- Find even ONE other neurodivergent person
- Build from there
- One genuine connection is better than none

Important reminders:

- You deserve community where you're understood
- Neurodivergent community isn't a replacement for neurotypical friendships, but it's a crucial addition

- You're not "not neurodivergent enough" to join—if you're neurodivergent, you belong
- It's okay to lurk before engaging
- First attempts at community might be awkward—that's normal
- Your tribe is out there—you just have to find them
- Community is what makes neurodivergence survivable and even joyful

Extension challenge:
Once you've found your community, help others find theirs:

- Welcome new members warmly
- Share community info with isolated neurodivergent people you meet
- Create content about your community experience to help others find connection
- Start or support neurodivergent student groups at your school

Every time you help someone find community, you strengthen the network for everyone.

Remember: You are not meant to navigate neurodivergence alone. Your people exist. Find them.

13

CONCLUSION

You've just read twelve stories about neurodivergent teens navigating a world that wasn't built for their brains. Twelve different people with twelve different struggles, strengths, and paths to self-understanding.

Maybe you saw yourself in Emma, learning to unmask after years of exhausting performance. Or in Marcus, realizing that his timeline doesn't have to match anyone else's. Maybe you connected with Jayden's struggle to build systems that work with his ADHD brain, or Kai's journey to create a sensory-safe space in an overwhelming world.

Perhaps Priya's fight for accommodations resonated with you, or Devon's passion for his special interest felt familiar. Maybe Aria's confusion about social scripts matched your own experience, or Sofia's diagnosis moment brought up complex emotions about your own neurodivergence.

You might have recognized yourself in Carlos reclaiming his stims, Nina recovering from burnout, Alex bridging the understanding gap with her parents, or Liam finding his tribe in the neurodivergent community.

Or maybe you saw pieces of yourself in all of them—because

being neurodivergent isn't a single experience. It's a spectrum of different brains, different challenges, different strengths, and different stories.

But here's what connects all twelve stories, and what connects you to every neurodivergent person who's ever felt different, misunderstood, or like they're operating on hard mode:

You are not broken. You are not too much. You are not failing at being human.

Your brain works differently. And that difference comes with real challenges—executive function struggles, sensory overwhelm, social confusion, emotional intensity, burnout risk, and a world that constantly demands you perform neurotypicality.

But it also comes with real strengths—deep focus, pattern recognition, honest communication, intense passion, creative problem-solving, and the ability to see the world from perspectives others miss.

What You've Learned

Through these twelve stories, you've explored:

The reality of masking and why you can't sustain performing neurotypicality forever without burning out. You've learned that unmasking is a process, not an event, and that finding spaces where you can be authentically yourself is essential for survival.

The danger of comparing yourself to neurotypical timelines and the freedom that comes from accepting your own pace. You've seen that developmental milestones, career paths, and life trajectories don't have to match anyone else's schedule.

The necessity of external systems and accommodations because willpower and trying harder don't fix executive function challenges or sensory sensitivities. You've learned that needing support isn't weakness—it's wisdom.

The importance of sensory self-advocacy and creating environments where your nervous system can actually regulate. You've seen that your sensory needs aren't preferences you should "get over"—they're real medical needs that deserve accommodation.

The power of self-advocacy and asking for what you need instead of suffering in silence. You've learned that accommodations aren't unfair advantages—they're access needs that level the playing field.

The value of special interests and deep focus in a world that often demands shallow engagement with everything. You've seen that passion and expertise matter more than being well-rounded.

The exhaustion of social navigation and the relief of finding people who communicate directly. You've learned that your straight-forward communication style is valuable, not deficient.

The complexity of diagnosis and the grief, relief, anger, and hope that come with finally understanding why everything has been so hard. You've seen that getting diagnosed is often the beginning of real change, not the end.

The right to stim and exist in your body without constantly suppressing your natural regulatory movements. You've learned that your stims aren't shameful behaviors to hide—they're essential self-care.

The reality of burnout and the absolute necessity of respecting your limits before your body forces you to. You've seen that rest isn't laziness—it's preventive medicine.

The importance of family understanding and finding ways to bridge the communication gap between neurodivergent needs and neurotypical assumptions. You've learned that education and translation can transform relationships.

The power of community and finding people who understand you without constant explanation. You've seen that connection with other neurodivergent people isn't just nice—it's necessary.

What Comes Next

You've finished the book, but your neurodivergent journey is just beginning—or continuing, if you've been on this path for a while.

So what do you do with everything you've learned?

First: Give yourself permission to be imperfect at this.

You're not going to suddenly unmask completely, set perfect boundaries, advocate flawlessly for your needs, and build an ideal support system overnight. This is a process. You'll make mistakes. You'll have setbacks. You'll have days when you mask hard because it feels safer, or when you push past your limits because you forget to listen to your body.

That's okay. Growth isn't linear. Healing isn't linear. Learning to accept and work with your neurodivergence instead of against it isn't linear.

Be patient with yourself.

Second: Start small and build incrementally.

You don't have to implement every strategy from every story right now. Pick ONE thing—one accommodation to request, one boundary to set, one system to build, one person to reach out to, one way to unmask, one limit to respect.

Start there. Build on it. Add more as you're ready.

Small changes compound over time. The tiny step you take today to honor your neurodivergent needs is the foundation for the bigger changes you'll make next month, next year, next decade.

Third: Find your people.

Community is not optional for neurodivergent people surviving in a neurotypical world. You need people who understand you without constant translation. People who share your experiences. People who celebrate your neurodivergence instead of just tolerating it.

Whether that's online communities, in-person meetups, neurodivergent friends at school, or even just one person who truly gets it— find your tribe. Seek them out actively. They exist, and they're looking for you too.

Fourth: Keep learning about yourself.

Your neurodivergence is uniquely yours. What works for Marcus might not work for you. Kai's sensory needs might be completely different from yours. Sofia's ADHD presentation might look nothing like your ADHD.

Pay attention to your patterns. Document what helps and what doesn't. Experiment with different strategies. Listen to your body and brain when they tell you what they need.

You are the expert on your own neurodivergence. Trust that expertise.

Fifth: Advocate for yourself—and for others.

The more you speak up about your needs, the easier it gets. The more you educate people about neurodivergence, the more understanding spreads. The more you normalize accommodations and unmasking and different communication styles, the safer the world becomes for the next neurodivergent person.

Your self-advocacy isn't just about you—it's about making space for everyone whose brain works differently.

When you ask for closed captions, you're making media more accessible for everyone who needs them.

When you stim openly, you're normalizing visible neurodivergence for the kid who's been hiding their stims in shame.

When you explain your communication style, you're teaching neurotypical people that there are valid ways to interact beyond their narrow scripts.

When you take time off for burnout recovery, you're modeling that rest is legitimate and necessary.

When you celebrate your special interests instead of hiding them, you're showing other neurodivergent people that passion is valuable.

Every time you honor your neurodivergent needs without apology, you make the world a little bit safer for all of us.

Sixth: Remember that your worth is not determined by productivity.

This is hard in a world that constantly tells you that your value comes from what you accomplish, how much you achieve, how well you perform.

But your worth is inherent. You don't have to earn the right to exist. You don't have to be "high-functioning" or successful or productive to deserve accommodation, compassion, and respect.

You are valuable because you exist. Period.

On the days when executive function fails and you can't start tasks, you're still valuable.

On the days when you're too overwhelmed to mask and you seem "more autistic" than usual, you're still valuable.

On the days when you need to rest instead of being productive, you're still valuable.

On the days when burnout means you can't do anything at all, you're still valuable.

Your neurodivergence is not something you have to overcome to be worthy of love and belonging. It's part of who you are—and who you are is enough.

The Hard Truth

I'm not going to lie to you: being neurodivergent in a neurotypical world is hard.

There will be days when masking feels unbearable but necessary. Days when no one understands what you're trying to explain. Days when sensory overload makes existing feel impossible. Days when executive function betrays you and you can't do basic tasks. Days when you're so tired of being different that you just want your brain to work like everyone else's.

There will be people who dismiss your needs as excuses. People who think accommodations are unfair advantages. People who tell you to just try harder, just focus more, just be normal. People who don't believe your struggles are real because you don't "look" disabled.

There will be systems that weren't designed for your brain and refuse to adapt. Schools that prioritize conformity over accessibility. Workplaces that demand neurotypical performance. Social spaces that punish visible neurodivergence.

The world is not set up for you. That's the truth.

But here's the other truth: **You are not alone. You are not the problem. And things are changing.**

There's a growing neurodivergent community—millions of people with ADHD, autism, dyslexia, and other brain differences—who are done with masking, done with shrinking themselves to fit neurotypical molds, done with being told they're broken.

We're building new spaces, new communities, new ways of existing that honor neurodivergent needs. We're educating neurotypical people about how our brains work. We're demanding accommodations and accessibility. We're rewriting the narrative about what it means to be neurodivergent.

The autistic adults, ADHD advocates, and neurodivergent activists who came before you fought hard to create the awareness, acceptance, and resources you have access to now. And you're going to continue that work—by existing authentically, by advocating for yourself, by supporting other neurodivergent people, by refusing to pretend your needs don't matter.

Change is slow. But it's happening. And you're part of it.

Your Neurodivergent Strengths

Before we end, I want to make sure you know this: your neurodivergence comes with real strengths that the world needs.

Your ADHD brain that struggles with sustained attention on boring tasks can also hyperfocus with intensity that produces incredible work. Your creativity, your ability to see connections others miss, your enthusiasm for things that interest you—those aren't despite your ADHD. They're because of it.

Your autistic brain that struggles with neurotypical social scripts can also communicate with honesty and authenticity that builds genuine connections. Your attention to detail, your pattern recognition, your deep expertise in your interests, your loyalty to people you care about—those aren't despite your autism. They're because of it.

Your dyslexic brain that struggles with traditional reading can also think spatially and creatively in ways that solve problems others can't. Your ability to see the big picture, your innovative thinking, your resilience from years of figuring out workarounds—those aren't despite your dyslexia. They're because of it.

Your neurodivergent brain is not a less-good version of a neurotypical brain. It's a different kind of brain with different strengths and different challenges.

Society has decided that neurotypical brains are "normal" and everything else is "disordered." But that's a social construct, not a truth. Your brain isn't wrong—it's just different. And different brings valuable perspectives, skills, and ways of being that the world desperately needs.

So yes, advocate for accommodations. Yes, ask for support. Yes, acknowledge the genuine struggles that come with being neurodivergent.

But also: celebrate your strengths. Own your differences. Take pride in your neurodivergence.

You're not broken. You're not less than. You're not a problem to be fixed.

You're neurodivergent. And that's something to be proud of.

IF YOU TAKE nothing else from this book, take this:

You deserve to exist as you are, not as a performance of what others expect you to be.

You deserve accommodations that let you function without destroying yourself.

You deserve relationships where you can communicate honestly without constant translation.

You deserve spaces where your sensory needs are respected, not dismissed.

You deserve time to rest without guilt about not being productive.

You deserve to stim, to info-dump about your interests, to struggle with things that others find easy, to need what you need without shame.

You deserve to take up space as your authentic neurodivergent self.

The twelve people in these stories learned—slowly, imperfectly, sometimes painfully—to honor their neurodivergent needs instead of constantly fighting against them. They learned to unmask, to advocate, to find community, to respect their limits, to build systems that worked with their brains instead of against them.

They learned that being neurodivergent wasn't something to overcome—it was something to understand, accommodate, and ultimately accept as a fundamental part of who they are.

You can learn that too.

It won't be easy. It won't be quick. But it's worth it.

Because you—the real, authentic, unmasked, beautifully neurodivergent you—are worth it.

Welcome to your neurodivergent journey. Your tribe is waiting. Your future is unwritten. Your brain is different, and that's exactly as it should be.

Go be spectacularly, unapologetically, authentically yourself.

The world needs your neurodivergent brain.

We're glad you're here.

Find all Richard Bass books at: amazon.com/author/richardbass **Connect with Richard:** YouTube channel "Thriving with Richard Bass"

Online Communities:

- Reddit: r/autism, r/ADHD, r/neurodiversity
- TikTok: Search #ActuallyAutistic, #ADHDTikTok, #Neurodivergent
- Discord: Many servers exist for neurodivergent teens (search for community invites)

Websites & Organizations:

- CHADD (Children and Adults with ADHD): chadd.org
- Autistic Self Advocacy Network: autisticadvocacy.org
- Understood.org (learning and thinking differences)
- ADDitude Magazine: additudemag.com

Mental Health Support: If you're in crisis:

- National Suicide Prevention Lifeline: 988
- Crisis Text Line: Text HOME to 741741
- Trevor Project (LGBTQ+ youth): 1-866-488-7386

Remember: These resources are starting points. Your therapist, school counselor, and local disability organizations may have additional resources specific to your area and needs.

You've got this.

ABOUT THE AUTHOR

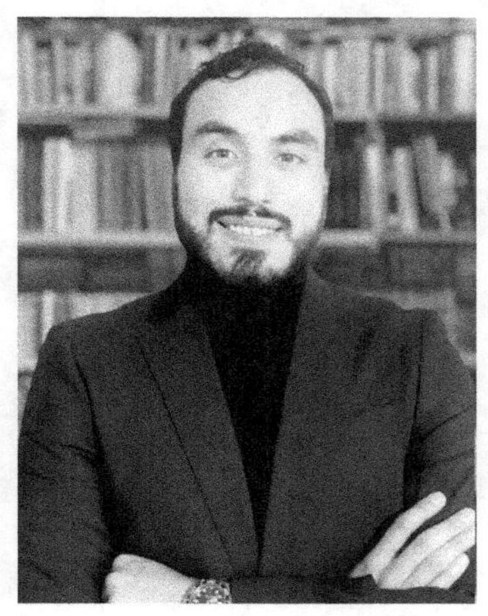 **Richard Bass** is a bestselling author and educator with over a decade of experience supporting children and teens with neurodivergence, anxiety, and depression. With more than 20 published books and workbooks, and over 100,000 copies sold, he provides parents and educators with practical, research-backed strategies that make a real impact.

Holding both bachelor's and master's degrees in education, along with certifications in Special Education (K–12) and Educational Administration, Richard blends academic knowledge with real-world insight to create tools that help children thrive emotionally, socially, and academically.

Richard connects with thousands of families through his YouTube channel, *Thriving with Richard Bass*, and regularly engages with his email community, offering encouragement, strategies, and evidence-based approaches. His work is grounded in meaningful dialogue with parents, teachers, and mental health professionals who are in the trenches every day.

A lifelong learner and avid traveler, Richard draws inspiration from global parenting and education styles to continually refine his approach. His mission is to promote empathy, understanding, and actionable solutions for children facing life's toughest challenges so every child has the chance to succeed.

Connect with Richard:

YouTube: Thriving with Richard Bass

Amazon: amazon.com/author/richardbass

Instagram, TikTok and Facebook: @richardbassauthor

Other Books in the Successful Parenting Series:

- The ADHD Parenting Guide for Boys & Girls
- Parenting a Child with Autism
- Beyond the Spectrum: A Guide to Parenting Adolescents With Autism
- The DBT Workbook for Teens
- And many more...